"I don't want anything to happen to you."

Daphne took that to heart. "Trust me, I feel the same way. But there are no guarantees, are there?" she stated honestly. "No woman wants to see her life come to an end by a serial killer. We can only try to outlast them while living our lives." She realized it wasn't as simple as that no matter how many times she said it. The female victims in her book were proof of that.

"You're right." Kenneth spoke calmly. "You can't hide under a rock. Just do me a favor—don't let your guard down, even as you live that life. If something were to ever upend it..."

His voice broke and Daphne instinctively reached across the table to touch his hand. "Don't worry. I'm not a quitter," she promised him. "I have so much to live for." *You're one of those things*, she thought, in spite of not knowing where they were headed.

In memory of my beloved mother, Marjah Aljean, a devoted lifelong fan of Harlequin romances, who inspired me to do my very best in finding happiness and success in my personal and professional endeavors. To H. Loraine, the love of my life, whose support has been unwavering through the many wonderful years together; and the loyal fans of my romance, mystery, suspense and thriller fiction published over the years.

Lastly, thanks to my fantastic editors, Allison Lyons and Denise Zaza, for the opportunity to lend my literary voice and creative spirit to the Harlequin Intrigue line.

DANGER ON MAUI

R. BARRI FLOWERS

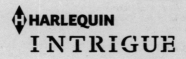

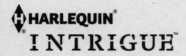

ISBN-13: 978-1-335-58249-2

Danger on Maui

Copyright © 2023 by R. Barri Flowers

For questions and comments about the quality of this book,
please contact us at CustomerService@Harlequin.com.

Harlequin Enterprises ULC
22 Adelaide St. West, 41st Floor
Toronto, Ontario M5H 4E3, Canada
www.Harlequin.com

Printed in U.S.A.

R. Barri Flowers is an award-winning author of crime, thriller, mystery and romance fiction featuring three-dimensional protagonists, riveting plots, unexpected twists and turns, and heart-pounding climaxes. With an expertise in true crime, serial killers and characterizing dangerous offenders, he is perfectly suited for the Harlequin Intrigue line. Chemistry and conflict between the hero and heroine, attention to detail and incorporating the very latest advances in criminal investigations are the cornerstones of his romantic suspense fiction. Discover more on popular social networks and Wikipedia.

Books by R. Barri Flowers

Harlequin Intrigue

Hawaii CI

The Big Island Killer
Captured on Kauai
Honolulu Cold Homicide
Danger on Maui

Chasing the Violet Killer

Visit the Author Profile page at Harlequin.com.

CAST OF CHARACTERS

Daphne Dockery—A bestselling true crime writer on Maui to research her next book, she enlists aid from a handsome detective who worked the case, while also trying to dodge a persistent stalker and being targeted by a serial killer at large.

Kenneth Kealoha—A homicide detective for the Maui PD Criminal Investigation Division, he's investigating a serial killer targeting attractive dark-haired women on the island. Can he stop the unsub from going after the Southern beauty who has captured his fancy?

Jared McDougall—An ex-cop and expert in criminal background analysis, living in retirement. But could he also be a serial killer?

Francis Hiraga—An ER doctor who is linked to both cases and may have knowledge pertinent to the current investigation.

Marissa Sheffield—An obsessed fan of Daphne's, who is intent on being in her life. But will the stalker go too far in her fixation on the true crime author?

The Maui Suffocation Killer—Terrorizing the island by suffocating his female victims to death. Will Daphne fall prey to his homicidal tendencies?

Prologue

He's hot, Jena Sutcliffe had to admit, as she admired from afar the tall, fit and handsome dark-haired man at Linc's Tavern on Wharf Street in Lahaina, a happening town in West Maui in the County of Maui, Hawaii. She doubted he even noticed her, even if most considered her to be attractive and a good catch, with long and luscious raven hair and pretty blue eyes. But Maui was full of good-looking and sexy young women, many of whom seemed to be at the club that night and were all over him like an expensive suit. Or was that just her imagination? Jena turned her focus to another dark-haired hottie, who was sitting at the bar all by his lonesome and, like her, appeared to be taking it all in, as if to size up both the competition and the hot women. Again, he never seemed to lay his eyes on her, as she apparently wasn't what he was looking for.

His loss, Jena told herself dismissively as she sipped her Lava Flow drink and pushed back at the thought of wanting to get the attention of Mr. Hot

Stuff. After all, what was it they said about the definition of insanity? Hadn't she already been burned in the past by tall, dark-haired, handsome and virile men who looked like him? Why put herself through that agony again?

Jena turned away from the man, content to finish off her drink and head home alone. She did need to get up early for work at a hotel, where she was an event planner. *Who knows, maybe I'll meet my sexy knight in shining armor at the next big event*, she told herself while not holding her breath. She made her way through the crowded bar, imagining one of the knights in shining armor would follow, sweep her off her feet, and it would be the start of something great.

By the time she left the place and climbed into her orange Subaru WRX, reality had set in and she drove home. Jena was unaware that someone had gotten into another vehicle and began to follow her.

IF HE HAD a dollar for every woman who never looked his way, underestimating him or just what he was capable of, he would be a very rich man right now. And then his true worth might be better appreciated. Until such time, he would allow his actions to speak for him and his victims would be forced to carry the brunt of it. Right to their early graves. And he would continue to have his revenge and take joy in the thrill of the kill. As well as the solace of knowing there was little that could be done to stop him. Not till he'd had enough of dishing out the type of pain that he had been given.

He followed the Subaru to a condominium complex on Lower Honoapiilani Road, allowing her to park first while pretending to be just another tenant coming home. Perhaps from a night out on the town, like her. Only his presence was much more sinister than that. Quickly parking, he left his vehicle and surreptitiously made his way inside the building. He happened to catch her scaling the stairwell and followed, noting she went to the third floor.

By the time he got there, he saw the door to her unit close. After making sure there were no prying eyes around, he walked up to the condo. Using his instincts that told him she was all by her lonesome, he rang the bell, calculating that she would at the very least be curious as to who he was. Hadn't that proven to be true time and time again? Gullibility was always their downfall. Why should it be any different on this occasion?

She did not fail, opening the door like clockwork and smiling at him as though greeting an old friend. "Can I help you?" she asked politely.

He grinned innocently and replied in a deceptive tone of voice, "Yes, I believe you can."

Using a stun gun, he placed it to her skin and she reacted accordingly with the electrical shocks doing a number to her body and brain, giving him complete control of his latest victim as he entered the condominium to finish what he'd so cleverly and joyously started.

Chapter One

At 10:00 a.m., Daphne Dockery sat on an uncomfortable wooden chair in the Aloha Land Bookstore on Front Street in Lahaina, pasting a perfect smile on her heart-shaped face as she signed copies of her latest bestselling book, *The Accident Killer*. As an award-winning true crime writer, Maui, Hawaii, was the last stop on a late summer book tour to push the unsettling real-life story of serial killer Oscar Preston, who made the deaths of his fifteen victims appear to be accidents till the frightening truth emerged and he was made to pay for his heinous crimes. Daphne planned to take full advantage of the idyllic setting in paradise for some much-needed rest and relaxation away from her hometown of Tuscaloosa, Alabama, after a difficult year that included a bad breakup with her ex-boyfriend, Nelson Holloway, and a scary encounter with an obsessed fan, Marissa Sheffield. Thankfully, Marissa was now in jail and Nelson probably should have been, given his unfaithfulness and questionable practices as a hedge-fund manager.

But Daphne hoped to put them behind her and focus on where she went from here as a newly single—but not necessarily looking for love and companionship—woman, thirty-two years of age, who had landed on Maui on a new mission. Apart from some fun in the sun and on the sand, along with taking a dip in the warm waters of the Pacific Ocean, she'd come to research her next book, tentatively titled *A Maui Mass Murder*. It was about a workplace love triangle on the island that resulted in a murder-suicide, taking the lives of five people last year, including a pregnant woman. The subject matter hit home for Daphne painfully. As an only child, her own father had snapped when her mother threatened to leave him and his abusive ways, resulting in him shooting her mother to death before turning the gun on himself.

Her own tragedy, when Daphne was only seven years old, set her on a course in which, as an adult, she wanted to delve into the backstory of violent criminals, criminality and victims to help others better understand the dynamics involved and learn to cope with it. After earning her Master of Arts degree in journalism and media studies from the University of Alabama and landing a job with a local news station as an investigative journalist, she needed greater autonomy to investigate hard-hitting stories and share them with the public on a larger scale.

Hence, she turned to writing true crime books and found success there with seven bestsellers to date and had contracted for three more books with her publisher. This included the next crime topic Daphne had chosen to write about and had been approved by her supportive editor, Gordon Yung, at Lefevre and Weigel Publishing.

But first, there's still the matter of wrapping up one more book signing for my current title, she thought, as Daphne glanced down at the fresh flower lei that hung over a scarlet-and-black-printed faux-wrap dress on her five-seven slender frame, worn with comfortable-to-walk-in moccasin flats. She again put on her best face and twinkled big blue-green eyes at the tall thirtysomething man with a medium build and dark hair in a mushroom cut. He was wearing a red shirt adorned with sunsets and palm trees and loose-fitting black jeans. Slightly crooked but intense brown eyes with flecks of gold were locked on hers as he held the hardcover book in big hands to his chest.

"Aloha." She spoke in a friendly voice, wanting to break the intensity of their staring game, as if to see who would blink first.

"Aloha." He kept his own voice level. "Welcome to Maui."

"Happy to be here." She wondered if he could say the same, judging by his anxious demeanor. *Better get this over with*, she thought, *and move on to someone less intimidating*. "Would you like me to sign your book?" Daphne assumed that to be the case, as he had waited in line rather than simply taking the book to the cashier to purchase.

"Yeah," he responded tersely, and handed it to her. "Make it out to Tommy."

"Okay." She used the pen the store provided and scribbled his name on the blank first page, followed by her usual words: *Thanks for taking the time to show up. Hope you find the read to your liking and pass it on to others interested in true crime. Daphne Dockery.*

She handed the book back to him and, in keeping up with Hawaiian lingo said lyrically, "Mahalo."

"Back at you," he said stiffly, and walked away.

Wouldn't want to get on his bad side, Daphne half joked to herself as the next person in line, a frail elderly woman with ash-colored hair worn in stacked layers approached. "Aloha."

"Aloha." Her face creased with a smile. "I'm a big fan of your books. In fact, I've read every single one of them."

Daphne blushed. "That's so nice to hear," she told her genuinely, never taking such comments for granted with so many books for readers to choose from out there.

"It's obvious that you put your heart and soul into each book."

"I try to," Daphne agreed, knowing this was what separated true crime narrative nonfiction books from criminology books, in essence. Being herself and freely prefacing each book with her own experience as a victim was what made her books popular and kept Daphne going as well in a cathartic sort of way. She took the book from her.

"You can make that out to Olivia Righetti."

"Will do." Daphne happily signed her book, feeling more confident that she wanted it for all the right reasons, as opposed to the last person perhaps.

"Hope you enjoy your stay on the island," Olivia said. "There's a lot more to do than being cooped up in a bookstore signing books, you know."

Daphne chuckled. "I promise to take some time to explore the sights, sounds and spirit of Maui."

The woman crinkled her eyes and took Daphne at her word, and Olivia gave a little wave as she walked off. Daphne took a sip of her bottled water on the table, which included stacks of books spread out strategically, as her throat felt dry from talking. Never mind that her hand was sore from signing books. But she would never complain about something that was part of the process for success as a top-selling author and remaining high on the best-seller lists for nonfiction.

"Nice to know you're up for taking in what the island has to offer," said a resonant voice that drew Daphne's attention. She looked up into the very deep brown-gray eyes of a chiseled face that belonged to a most handsome Hawaiian man. His curly black hair was in a textured fringe cut that went agreeably with the rest of him, which included at least a six-foot, three-inch sturdy frame and long legs. He was dressed in casual attire apropos of Hawaiian living, consisting of a tropical print shirt, dark straight-fit chino pants and brown Venetian loafers.

When she could get her mouth to move, Daphne chuckled and responded wryly, "I wouldn't have it any other way."

He grinned easily. "Good to hear."

As she tended to do when nervousness got the better of her, Daphne flipped her long and layered raven hair that was styled in a U-shaped cut. She managed to look past his good-looking face to the copy of her book he was holding. "Who do I make that out to?" she asked, if only to get back to the business at hand and not the man himself.

He slid the book across the table up to her. "Ken should be fine and whatever else you'd like to say that I can brag to my buddies about."

Daphne laughed, trying to imagine him bragging about having a signed copy of *The Accident Killer* to anyone. Somehow, he didn't seem the type to take such a thing too seriously. "You have yourself a deal," she quipped. "Ken and a bit more to say mahalo for coming in today."

"Wouldn't have missed the chance to pick up a signed copy of your latest true crime book as a serious fan of narrative nonfiction of this kind," he insisted.

"I see." *Guess my reach truly is far and wide, with a readership that apparently knows no bounds,* she told herself as she signed the book and handed it back to him, realizing there were others waiting in line before she could call it quits and move on to the rest of her important agenda while on Maui. "Hope it lives up to your expectations."

Ken grinned from one side of his wide mouth that appealed to her all on its own as perfectly kissable were the circumstances different and amenable. "I'm sure it will. Have a safe trip back to the mainland whenever you return."

"Thanks." Daphne smiled back and watched briefly as he headed to the cashier while wondering about his life story as, she assumed, an island resident. Was he single and available? Judging by his laidback clothing, trying to figure out what he did for a living was almost impossible, as in this tropical environment it could be anything from a business owner to a lecturer. Or maybe he was a resort worker or involved with technology. She supposed some things were best left to the imagination as Daphne welcomed the next book buyer before her, happy to see the line was starting to thin. Which meant she would soon be able to get the most out of her stay on the island, including her investigation into the mass shooting at the workplace.

HOMICIDE DETECTIVE KENNETH KEALOHA, a member of the Maui Police Department's Criminal Investigation Division branch of the Investigative Services Bureau, couldn't seem to get his mind off Daphne

Dockery, the stunning true crime writer he met earlier in the day at her book signing. In fact, if the truth be told, she looked even better in person than the photograph on the back of her book, *The Accident Killer*, which he fully intended to read with interest. But he couldn't actually relay that to her in front of other book buyers, lest she get the impression he was trying to hit on her. Another place, another time, that might not have been too far from Kenneth's mind, as she was definitely his type with the luscious and long dark hair, enticing aquamarine eyes and streamlined physique. But in this instance, he thought it was probably best that he kept this view of the gorgeous author to himself.

As for her true crime book, given the subject matter involving a serial killer named Oscar Preston, who murdered fifteen people ten years ago in Mobile, Alabama, and was suspected of killing ten others, Kenneth was admittedly curious about her take on the ruthless killer who was given the moniker the "Accident Killer" and his ultimate capture and conviction. It was that same year that another serial killer, Trevor Henshall, operating out of Honolulu, Hawaii, and dubbed the "Paradise Foot Killer" strangled to death ten women in some twisted foot fetish and fixation on their beach walks. One of those women, Cynthia Suehisa, was a close friend of Kenneth's. Like him, Cynthia was a native Hawaiian who'd had her whole life ahead of her before it was snuffed out like a candle's bright flame. At the time, he was a detective for the Honolulu Police Department's Criminal Investigation Division, investigating crimes of violence. In spite of killing Henshall when he refused to surrender, Kenneth had been unable to prevent his friend from becoming a murder victim, dying in his arms.

Two years later, Kenneth transferred to the Maui PD, as much for a fresh start as to put the darkness of Cynthia's untimely death behind him to the extent possible. He had learned the hard way that crime would follow him wherever he went as a police detective tasked with going after bad people. At thirty-three, with no love life to distract him, his sole focus these days was pretty much solving serious crimes to the best of his ability. With homicides topping the list.

That included his current investigation. A serial killer was terrorizing attractive women with long dark hair on the island of Maui. Nicknamed by the local press the "Maui Suffocation Killer," the unsub suffocated his victims to death by putting a plastic bag over their heads and faces. Thus far, nine unlucky women had been murdered due to asphyxia over the past eight months. The last one, Jena Sutcliffe, met her fate a week ago. Another woman, Ruth Paquin, was nearly killed around the time of the third fatality but managed to survive the attack. Unfortunately, due to the brain injury she suffered, all she could tell them was that the killer was a dark-haired male, maybe of medium build, with only a vague description beyond that. Using what they had in trying to piece it together, a task force had zeroed in on a suspect.

Zack Lawrence was a thirty-eight-year-old fitness instructor and self-described ladies' man. He also happened to have been present at all the bars the victims had been seen at the night they were killed. Though there was no solid evidence to make an arrest, there was reason to believe Lawrence could be the man they were after. Starting with a prior conviction for attempting to smother to death an ex-girlfriend. Then there was the fact that he had been trying to date at least one of the victims, but was apparently rebuffed by her.

At the moment, they hoped to catch him in the act. Or at least an attempted act of abduction and murder. Which was why they were currently conducting an evening stakeout of the suspect at Popi's Tavern on Lower Main Street in the town of Wailuku, the county seat and commercial hub of Maui County. Kenneth was undercover at a table across from Detective Tad Newsome. At thirty, between his perpetual tan, lean frame, blue eyes, and short blondish-brown hair in an undercut style, he could easily have passed for a surfer instead of a cop, Kenneth believed. They pretended to be sipping Mai Tais, which was actually only orange juice.

At another table were FBI agents Kirk Guilfoyle and Noelle Kaniho, giving the guise of being a loving couple. In reality, at forty-five with a shaven bald head and landing strip goatee, Guilfoyle, African American with coal black eyes, was ten years older and happily married to his high school sweetheart; while Noelle had a longtime boyfriend and looked younger than her age with short and cropped blond hair and brown eyes behind fake vintage glasses. Kenneth nodded to them, making sure everyone was on the same page, before directing his attention to the bar, where working undercover as the decoy was Detective Vanessa Ringwald. The twenty-five-year-old green-eyed, single mother fit the prototype of the Maui Suffocation Killer's victims. She was slender and attractive with long and layered dark curly hair and baby bangs, that would normally have been worn in a high ponytail while on duty. She had on a sexy multicolored flare dress and strap sandals in doing her part to get the suspect to make his move.

Kenneth peered at Zack Lawrence, who was sitting beside Vanessa. The suspect was about his own height of just under six-three and every bit as in shape, with blue eyes, an oval face, and dark brown hair worn in a skin fade comb-over style. *I suppose I could see why women might be attracted to the man*, Kenneth mused, taking a sip of the orange juice. The only question was whether, like the Pied Piper, he led them down a road from which there was no coming back.

When Vanessa gave the signal that Lawrence appeared to swallow the bait and that they were leaving together, Kenneth acknowledged this. Stressed, he made sure that the other undercover law enforcement personnel knew what was about to go down. That included texting the detectives who were hanging around outside in case they were needed as backup.

"Get ready to head out," Kenneth informed Newsome.

"Ready when you are," he responded eagerly.

As Vanessa and Lawrence walked past them, with the suspect having a territorial hand on the small of her back, Kenneth waited till the last possible moment to follow and set things in motion. Outside, they allowed the suspect to lead Vanessa across the fairly well-lit parking lot to his car, a silver Porsche 718 Boxster Convertible, where they hoped to find the tools of his trade for smothering his victims before swinging into action, and Lawrence appeared to try to kiss the detective on the passenger side. She turned her face at the last moment, with the kiss hitting Vanessa's chin.

Law enforcement converged on the two before Lawrence could get Vanessa into the car. Kenneth had his department issued Glock 17 semi-automatic pistol out and aimed at the suspect's shocked face. Just as he was about to come to Vanessa's rescue, she had turned Lawrence around, twisted his arm and handcuffed him roughly while announcing in a confident and harsh tone, "Detective Ringwald, Maui PD. You're under arrest."

Lawrence, who looked flustered, was defiant. "For what? Wanting to get together with what I believed to be a like-minded pretty woman who came on to me only to try to entrap me?"

"You did that all on your own," she insisted with a snap. "Did you really think you could charm me with your empty words?"

"Not a chance," Kenneth quipped, approaching her. "She's not nearly that easy."

"You've got that right." Vanessa made a comical face at him. "What took you so long, Kealoha? For a moment there, I thought I was going to have to take a ride with this creep."

Kenneth chuckled, knowing it would never have come to that. He placed his firearm back in its leather holster. "Since you seemed to have things well under control, we took our own sweet time." He turned the suspect around to face him and stuck a search warrant in the pocket of his blazer. "This gives us the right to take a look inside your car."

Lawrence scowled. "Go ahead. Look all you want. As I've said all along, I've got nothing to hide."

"We'll see about that," Kenneth countered, hopeful they had found their perp before he could do any more damage. "Don't move," he warned him, though it was clear that Vanessa and the others had the upper hand in keeping the suspect from even thinking about fleeing.

Putting on a pair of nitrile gloves, Kenneth took a look inside the Porsche, searching for anything incriminating that might link Lawrence to the serial killings. Regrettably, he found nothing, but would leave it to the crime scene technicians to dig deeper. When emerging from the vehicle, Kenneth noted a frown on the face of Detective Tad Newsome, who said, "We may have a problem."

"What is it?" he asked anxiously.

"Just got the call. A young woman's body was discovered by her neighbor in Kahului. It looks like she was a victim of foul play in a manner reminiscent of the Maui Suffocation Killer's victims. The neighbor reported seeing a man, fitting the general description of the serial killer, fleeing from the residence." Newsome ran a hand across his jaw, glancing at the suspect. "Lawrence may not be our guy, after all."

"What a shock." Lawrence rolled his eyes sarcastically, then narrowed them at Kenneth. "Sorry to disappoint."

Though frustrated, Kenneth had to admit he was thinking the same thing regarding the guilt of the suspect. Or lack thereof. Given that they had been surveilling the fitness instructor ever since he left the gym on Kolu Street in Wailuku, Zack Lawrence just might have bought his ticket to freedom. Unless he had crossed the line with Vanessa and she chose to press charges on something akin to assault on a law enforcement officer. Still, he hated giving the smug suspect the pleasure of knowing they had screwed up. But the reality was that Lawrence could well be innocent as a serial murderer. "We'll hold on to Mr. Lawrence for the time being," Kenneth ordered while Vanessa pondered the notion, to be on the safe side.

Even then, Kenneth had a sinking feeling that the real unsub had struck again while their attention was occupied elsewhere.

Twenty-five minutes later, this had been more or less confirmed as Kenneth stood in the crime scene—a spacious bedroom in a single-story mission-style house on Mokapu Street in Kahului, a town in central Maui that was home to the Kahului Harbor and main airport in Maui County. The Hawaiian victim was identified as Irene Ishibashi, a thirty-one-year-old fashion designer. Between traditional furnishings, she was lying atop a cotton quilt on a platform bed, fully clothed in a blue square-neck dress and mules. Long black hair in a mermaid style surrounded a narrow face, marred by the clear plastic bag covering it, her features distorted grotesquely as she undoubtedly fought desperately for air that fell far short of what was needed for survival. One of the two plush pillows was beside the body with facial impressions that suggested it may have been used by her attacker in the aftermath of the suffocation to further ensure its success. As there was no sign of forced entry, Kenneth believed that the victim had likely opened the door voluntarily to her attacker, either recognizing the person or doing what way too many people did naturally when someone rang the bell. Opened the door first and asked questions later. Only in this instance, there would be no later for Irene Ishibashi.

"What's your take on this?" Kenneth almost

dreaded to ask as the Maui County medical examiner and coroner did a preliminary examination of the victim.

Dr. Rudy Samudio was brown-eyed, thin, and in his sixties, but barely had any gray in his short raven hair in a pompadour cut. Wearing latex gloves, he removed the plastic bag from the dead woman's head, then turned her face from side to side as if a rag doll before responding bleakly, "My initial assessment is that the decedent died from asphyxia, almost certainly as a result of that plastic bag cutting off the flow of oxygen to the brain."

Kenneth sighed. "I was afraid you'd say that, but not really surprised, considering."

Samudio pointed to what appeared to be small burns on the deceased's neck. "It looks like the killer used a stun gun on the victim."

"Suspected as much," Kenneth said, recognizing the signs.

Samudio wrinkled his thick nose. "I'd say the so-called Maui Suffocation Killer has struck again with a nasty vengeance," he said flatly.

That too pretty much went without saying as Kenneth wrestled with the stark reality that the unsub had been anything but brought to his knees. Quite the contrary, he had once more managed to kill and evade capture. For now. Allowing the Crime Scene Response Team to take over in searching for evidence, Kenneth left the home that, by all appearances, seemed orderly in spite of the homicide that had taken place there. This suggested to him that the methodical serial killer was, as before, quick and decisive in his actions, taking care not to create disorder where not needed to carry out his crime.

"We need to cut Zack Lawrence loose," Kenneth informed Vanessa outside near some fishtail palm trees and landscape lighting, where she had been interviewing the neighbor who reported the crime, an elderly widow named Mary Cabanilla, before an officer escorted her away. "He's not our serial killer."

"I gathered that." Vanessa had put her hair back into her customary ponytail. "Especially after taking Mrs. Cabanilla's statement. According to her, when she saw a man dart out of the victim's front door and hightail it down the street, Mrs. Cabanilla sensed something was up and went to check on her neighbor, only to find Irene Ishibashi dead. The witness provided a description of the man she saw running away. Not precise, but slightly different from the surviving victim's portrayal of her attacker, which we can blame on her brain injury."

"That gives us something to work with," Kenneth said matter-of-factly, planning to have a sketch artist drop by to see Mary Cabanilla.

Vanessa drew a breath. "As for Zack Lawrence, he's definitely arrogant and annoying, but apparently not a killer. He's just a heartbreaker for gullible women. But not me," she emphasized.

"Didn't think so." Kenneth managed a grin. He'd heard that she was starting to see someone outside the force, but did not pry. Any more than she had about his pretty much nonexistent love life these days, though not from lack of wanting to find that special someone who got him and vice versa. But he wouldn't force the issue. If it happened, it happened. If not, then he guessed it just wasn't in the cards for him. "Other women might do well to run as far away from the man as possible."

"I'm with you there," she agreed, and argued emphatically, "I'd say the same for any women unfortunate enough to come into the crosshairs of the Maui Suffocation Killer. Assuming they lived to talk about it."

Kenneth's lips became a thin line. "Yeah, there is that," he conceded, knowing that only one, thus far, had escaped death at the serial killer's hands. "With any luck, we'll catch the unsub before he can add to his list of victims."

"Right." Her face expressed doubt. "Until then, we'll stay on it."

"Yeah." Kenneth gave a determined nod and watched as Vanessa went to confer with Detective Tad Newsome and FBI agents Guilfoyle and Kaniho. Kenneth took out his cell phone, knowing it was up to him to try and explain to the Assistant Chief of Investigative Services Bureau, Martin Morrissey, how the stakeout of Zack Lawrence had gone awry while the real killer was targeting another victim.

Chapter Two

Daphne was up early in the Kiki Shores luxury oceanfront villa on Kai Malina Parkway in Kaanapali. The beautiful and popular resort was on the west shore of Maui. As much as she would have liked to have slept in for another hour or so in the comfortable king-sized bed in the large primary bedroom, with a second bedroom serving as her temporary office, that would have to wait for another day. There were things to do and people to see, one in particular. Having done her research, Daphne had found out that the lead investigator in the murder-suicide case she was working on was a homicide detective named Kenneth Kealoha. From experience, she had learned that interviewing detectives working the investigations provided just the right context needed to ensure the true crime book balanced in its factual basis and verisimilitude while keeping the readers engaged throughout. *Hopefully, Detective Kealoha will be cooperative and not just blow me off,* she thought while tying her hair up.

After putting on a blue T-shirt and gray shorts, Daphne stepped into a new pair of white running shoes, ready to break them in. She spotted a small gecko on the cream-colored wall as she passed beneath the swirling fern-leaf ceiling fan and across the villa's ceramic tile flooring. Moving past the vintage furnishings with a modern feel, she headed out for a quick morning run on Kaanapali Beach. It included three miles of pristine golden white sand and an endless view of the clear waters of the deep blue ocean. Then there was Black Rock, the hot spot on the nearshore for cliff diving. She wondered if she could muster up the courage to give it a try during her stay. Beyond that, she could see the Hawaiian islands of Lanai and Molokai. There were a few other runners out, but well spaced from one another. One tall and tanned male runner acknowledged her before picking up speed, as if to show off his powerful legs. She chuckled within. *At least I can be myself here and not be bothered by anyone*, Daphne mused, knowing full well that being somewhat of a celebrity—at least in Tuscaloosa—was not all it was cracked up to be. Attracting the wrong attention could become a nightmare as thoughts of her stalker, Marissa Sheffield, filled Daphne's head.

She shut this down, determined not to give in to an ordeal that was now over. Once back in the villa, she took a shower, dressed and grabbed a bite to eat at the Kiki Shores restaurant. Then Daphne got in her rented Chevy Malibu, equipped with a GPS naviga-

tion system, and used the voice directions to make
her way to the Maui Police Department on Mahalani
Street in Wailuku.

At the front desk, Daphne was told by the thirtysomething burly male desk officer where to find
Detective Kenneth Kealoha. When she reached his
cubicle, there was a tall and dark-haired man standing by a wooden desk with his back to her. Clearing
her throat to get his attention, Daphne uttered, "I'm
looking for Detective Kealoha…"

The man turned around and locked solid brown-
gray eyes with her, looking just as shocked as she
was. "You found him," he said equably.

"Ken." The word blurted out of Daphne's mouth
even before she began to put the pieces together in
sizing up the man she'd met yesterday at her book
signing.

"Daphne Dockery, the true crime writer," he said
in return, an amused grin playing on his full mouth.
"Ken is short for Detective Kenneth Kealoha, which
I'm sure you've probably already figured out."

She blushed. "I gathered that much."

"Feel free to stick with Ken, if you like." Kenneth
stared at her and stuck out his hand. "Have to say, I
didn't think we'd see each other again. At least not
so soon." He laughed wryly as they shook hands.

"Neither did I," she had to admit, having no idea
of who he was the first time around, while feeling
the sensations of their skin contact.

"You're not stalking me, are you?" he asked playfully.

"Not funny." Daphne made a face. She considered stalking serious business, having been a victim of it.

Kenneth seemed to pick up on her uneasiness with the subject matter. "Poor choice of words," he said contritely. "Sorry about that." He paused. "So, what can I do for you?"

Daphne smoothed a thin eyebrow. "I need your help," she said tentatively, commanding his contemplation. "Or to get some information from you."

"Go on," he prodded gently.

She took a breath. "I'm writing a book about the murder-suicide involving the Takahashi family that took place on the island last summer. Since you were the lead detective on the case, I was hoping to talk to you about it to help fill in some of the blanks."

"I see." Kenneth shifted his weight to one leg. "As much as I'd love to help you, Ms. Dockery, right now I'm in the middle of a major investigation."

"Please call me Daphne," she told him, sensing that it had suddenly seemed to become more formal between them. But she didn't come there simply to be turned away. Not without giving it her all. "I understand that you're busy, Ken," she allowed in a friendly voice, "but I just need a little bit of your time. I can pay you…"

He frowned. "I don't want your money."

Did I just insult him unintentionally, or what? Daphne asked herself. "Perhaps this was a bad idea," she said. "I'll just have to work my way around this part. Maybe you could direct me to one of the other detectives who was involved in the investigation?"

Kenneth met her eyes and she could tell he was having second thoughts. "I'm probably your best bet to get what you need," he spoke evenly. "And while we're at it, I have a few questions of my own for you."

"Oh...?" She cocked a brow curiously, wondering if his questions were professional. Or more of a personal nature?

He didn't follow up on that, instead asking, "Can we get together this afternoon, maybe for lunch?"

"That works for me," Daphne agreed, perhaps too eagerly. "Lunch is a good time to talk." Especially if they could do so at a relatively quiet place.

Kenneth concurred. "Where are you staying?" She told him, knowing it was asked for the right reasons, coming from the handsome detective, who then said, "I can meet you at the Seas Grill in Whalers Village at one."

"I'll see you there," she said, knowing of the swanky outdoor shopping center on Kaanapali Beach, having already acquainted herself with it during a walkthrough.

He grinned crookedly. "Look forward to it."

"Me, too." Daphne smiled back, wishing she wasn't so attracted to him, if only to keep her focus on the mission at hand. But then again, she saw no harm in admiring the detective, who seemed to be just as taken with her, even while remaining somewhat aloof.

Kenneth walked her out halfway, introducing her to some of his colleagues along the way. Daphne could tell that they had each other's backs in the tough world of law enforcement, which was important in being able to solve cases and stay on the same page along the way. While she didn't necessarily have that type of almost-familial bond as a writer, Daphne did have a close relationship with her editor, Gordon, and some others at her publisher. She hoped to someday be able to find it again on an intimate level, but was not about to get ahead of herself in the process.

BEFORE THEY WENT their separate ways, Kenneth gave Daphne the once-over and admitted that she was just as stunning as when he first laid eyes on her the day before. Maybe even better when she wasn't half hidden behind a table, so he could take in her tall and slender physique in a white eyelet top with puffed sleeves, slim-leg stone-colored pants and dark double-zip booties to go with the good looks and stylishly long dark hair. What was he thinking in nearly passing up the opportunity to get to see her again? Yes, he was busy with the serial killer case they were all under pressure to solve. But not so much that he couldn't give some of his time to help the bestselling author with her latest book. Having had a front-row seat in the investigation of Norman Takahashi—who murdered his pregnant wife, mother-in-law, teenage daughter, and her boyfriend before killing himself—

Kenneth could certainly provide some details that would undoubtedly strengthen the book's credibility.

Besides that, he realized that Daphne could be of benefit to him as well with her previous title. Writing about another serial killer might have given her some insight that he could tap into in his current investigation. Having an opportunity to get to know the striking writer a bit better was something Kenneth could hardly afford to pass up as a bonus. When he got back to his desk, he got on his laptop for a cursory background check on Daphne Dockery ahead of their sit-down. Googling her, he saw that she was thirty-two, from Tuscaloosa, Alabama, lost her parents at an early age as an only child, gotten a master's degree in journalism and media studies from the University of Alabama and worked as an investigative journalist for a local news station before authoring seven international bestsellers. In celebrity status news, he noted that Daphne had split from her wealthy and older boyfriend, Nelson Holloway, seven months ago. Apparently, no one had taken his place in her life since.

He must have been a jerk or flat-out crazy to have let her slip away, Kenneth thought, feeling that Daphne was someone he could imagine fighting tooth and nail to hang on to, had they been together. But then he couldn't get into the head of her ex or Daphne, for that matter, to know what drove them apart. Given his own shortcomings in the relationship department, he wasn't exactly in a position to make judgment calls on others. Right now, he would settle for spending a little time with Daphne before she headed back to Alabama.

Shortly before 1:00 p.m., Kenneth pulled his department-issued dark sedan into the Whalers Village parking lot on Kaanapali Parkway. He walked to the Seas Grill restaurant and saw Daphne standing near the door when he arrived. "Aloha."

"Aloha," she said back, adding before he could ask, "No, I haven't been waiting long."

"Good." He gave her a sheepish smile while opening the door and they went inside. After being seated by the window, Kenneth looked at the menu and said, "I'm starving. See anything that looks interesting to an Alabamian?"

"Everything, actually." Daphne chuckled and studied her menu before settling on an organic Caesar salad and fish taco.

"Good choices," he said, and went with the chopped garden salad, fries and a cheeseburger. Both ordered fresh lemonade. "So, what would you like to know about the Takahashi family mass murder?" Kenneth decided to get right to it, troubling as it was to have to relive the tragedy that rocked Maui last year.

Daphne pulled a voice recorder out of her hobo handbag. "Do you mind?"

"Please do," Kenneth said, wanting as much as her to ensure accuracy if he was to be quoted for the book.

She cut the recorder on and asked without prelude,

"What drove Norman Takahashi to commit this hor-rific act of violence?"

Kenneth took a breath thoughtfully. "Simply put, jealous homicidal rage. Takahashi, forty-six, an as-sociate professor in the University of Hawaii Maui College's Mathematics Department, learned that his thirty-eight-year-old wife, Jenny, was carry-ing another man's child and wanted out of the mar-riage. This apparently caused Takahashi to go off the deep end at the couple's home. He used a 20-gauge pump-action shotgun to mow down his wife, the couple's eighteen-year-old daughter, Sarah, her twenty-year-old boyfriend, Lucas Piimauna, and Jen-ny's sixty-two-year-old mother, Donna Duldulao. Then Takahashi used a .22 Magnum revolver to shoot himself fatally in the head."

Daphne cringed. "What a shame," she muttered sadly.

"Tell me about it," he concurred.

"Did the weapons belong to Takahashi?"

Kenneth lifted his chin and nodded. "Yes, he had a permit for both firearms and they were registered with the Maui PD."

"Oh, that makes it all the more tragic," she said with a catch to her voice.

"Yeah. We can always debate about more gun con-trol legislation, but at the end of the day if someone is hell-bent on doing something like this, the firearms are accessible, legal or not."

"So true." She paused. "Did alcohol or drugs play a role in Takahashi's actions?"

"Most likely. According to the toxicology report, there were excessive amounts of alcohol and fentanyl in his system at the time of the murder-suicide."

"Figures." Daphne gave him a knowing look. "Still, losing it like that through gun violence, whatever the triggers, and ending the lives and futures of the victims, including himself, boggles the mind."

Kenneth had to agree. "It never gets any easier having to investigate these types of crimes. Not to say that murder-suicide is all that common on the island. But it does occur, even in paradise." He stopped and looked at her. "Of course, you already know this, since that's what brought you to Maui. Along with your book signing."

She acknowledged as much with her expression. "I only wish it had been under better circumstances, apart from the signing. But this is what comes with the territory in writing true crime books. It's something I believe I was meant to do."

Kenneth knew he didn't have the full story of her background, having skimmed over her prefaces. After the food arrived, and she stopped recording, he inquired further, "What got you into writing nonfiction books on crime?"

Daphne's voice shook as she answered, "My dad killed my mom, before putting the gun up to his own head and committing suicide. I was seven at the time and had to be taken in by an aunt. Lovable as Aunt Mae was, life wasn't quite the same from that point on"

"I'm sorry to hear that." This had to have affected her in ways Kenneth could not imagine. Losing both parents at such a young age was something he wouldn't wish on his worst enemy, given the normal stresses young people dealt with growing up.

"I suppose I knew then that I wanted to do something with my life to address violent crime in all its ugliness and help people to better deal with it to one degree or another."

"Seems like you've succeeded," he pointed out, lifting his cheeseburger. "I've seen some of the reviews of your books and it appears as if readers are all in for whatever story you choose to dig into."

"Thanks." She blushed while forking lettuce from the Caesar salad. "We all have our calling. It's up to us to try to do the best we can with that."

"True enough."

Daphne tasted the lemonade and asked, "So, what drew you into becoming a detective?"

Kenneth wiped his mouth. "I've been asked that a time or two." He sat back musingly, sipping his own lemonade. "Guess I've had an interest in law enforcement for as long as I can remember," he said. "After getting a bachelor's degree in criminology and criminal justice at Chaminade University of Honolulu, I ended up working for the Honolulu PD. I've been with the Maui PD for the last eight years."

"Living on Maui obviously agrees with you." She

laughed. "Of course, who wouldn't like being in this oasis day in and day out?"

"Maybe you should give it a try yourself," he tossed out jokingly, assuming she was happy living in Alabama. "Yes, it can be a paradise, excluding the times when it's not."

"Well, there is that," she conceded with a chuckle. "Still, I could probably get used to the constant sunshine and nice weather, gorgeous beaches, swaying palm trees and the like."

And I could get used to having you around to get to know on a deeper level, Kenneth told himself honestly, but didn't go there, believing it to be unlikely that she would stay once her research was completed. No reason to set himself up for disappointment. On the other hand, there was nothing preventing them from friendship or whatever on a short-term basis. "Do you have more questions for me?" he asked coolly.

"I do," Daphne confessed, and turned her recorder back on. "What can you tell me about the man Jenny Takahashi was involved with?"

Kenneth sat back. "His name is Francis Hiraga. They were physician colleagues at the Maui Medical Center. Hiraga, an ER doctor, had apparently hoped to marry Takahashi and raise their child together. At the time of her murder, Hiraga was at a medical conference on Kauai, and was cleared of any involvement in the crime."

"And yet he was involved, in spite of the separation," she pointed out remorsefully, "having to live with the what-ifs for the rest of his life."

"Yeah, that's true," Kenneth said, sensing Daphne was reliving the death of her parents. He, too, found himself relating to this sense of loss in his own life with the death of someone he was close to.

When it was his turn again to ask the questions, Kenneth paid for the lunch and they went outside and sat on a bench beside a cluster of bamboo palm trees. It was there that he recounted the murder of his friend, Cynthia Suehisa, by a serial killer in Honolulu, the same year that Oscar Preston, the subject of Daphne's book *The Accident Killer*, was committing serial murders in Mobile, Alabama.

"I'm so sorry to hear about your friend," Daphne expressed.

"Though it was a long time ago," Kenneth admitted mournfully, "it still hurts." He sighed. "In any event, your book about Preston interested me, as much for its parallels to the Honolulu serial killer case as a current set of murders on Maui I'm investigating, thought to be the work of a serial killer."

"Really?" Her eyes grew wide. "I've been so consumed with my book signing and research that I didn't even pick up on this. Tell me more…"

Knowing he wasn't compromising the investigation with basic information, Kenneth said, "He's been dubbed by the press as the Maui Suffocation Killer, as the unsub kills his victims, who are all attractive dark-haired women who were at a nightclub prior to their death, by suffocating them. So far, there have been ten victims that we know of." Even in so saying, Kenneth couldn't help but think that Daphne herself fit the profile of the dead women. Did she contemplate this as well?

Blinking, while otherwise remaining poised, she said evenly, "Sounds like something that would make a great true crime book, once the killer has been brought to justice."

"I suppose so," he acknowledged, considering this was her forte. "Which brings me to your last book."

"What would you like to know?"

In that moment, they brushed shoulders and Kenneth felt an electric shock surge through him. He assumed she felt it, too. Pushing that aside, he confessed, "I haven't started reading it yet, but since you've written about a serial killer, what's your view on what makes them tick that might provide some insight into the mind of the Maui killer on the loose?"

Daphne paused while meeting his eyes. "Well, in the case of Oscar Preston, he got a pathological thrill out of fooling the authorities and public into believing the murders he committed were accidents—be it by drowning, falling from a high-story building, tinkering with brakes and other means. It was only when the dots were connected and it told a different story, that it led to Preston's downfall. But, based on Preston and other serial killers I've written about, the common denominator appears to be a lust for killing, often fueled by hatred and rage, along with favorable circumstances that lowers the risk for identification and capture."

Kenneth nodded. "That seems to fall in line with my way of thinking," he told her. "While we haven't been able to nail down the specifics of the Maui Suffocation Killer's motivation, it's a good bet that the victims are being targeted based on physical characteristics and opportunity."

"I agree," she said. "And knowing I fit the bill, doesn't make me particularly comfortable at the moment."

"Nor should you be," he told her bluntly, believing that this knowledge could well save her life, should it come to that. "Being on your guard for anyone acting suspicious while on the island is probably a good idea, just to be on the safe side."

"Now that you mention it, there was a man at the book signing yesterday who kind of gave me the creeps."

"Oh...?" Kenneth gazed at her. "How so?"

"Nothing I can really put a finger on," Daphne said. "It's just the way he was checking me out, as if sizing me up for the kill." She laughed. "Likely nothing more than the overactive imagination of a true crime writer. He was probably harmless."

"Probably." Kenneth wondered what the odds were that the serial killer would come to a book signing for a book about a serial killer. Sounded crazy. But stranger things had happened. Hadn't they? "Do you remember what he looked like?"

"Not so much," she admitted. "There were a lot of books signed, yours included, making the faces and body shapes almost a blur after a while. He was just a regular guy. Though I would probably recognize him if I saw him again."

"Hopefully, you never will," Kenneth told her. "If only because he rubbed you the wrong way, which may be worth missing a book sale."

Daphne chuckled. "You're right about that."

He took out his cell phone and Kenneth realized the time had gotten away from him. In spite of enjoying this, he said reluctantly, "I have to get going."

"Me, too." She stood first. "Once you finish reading *The Accident Killer*, if you have any other questions, I'll be happy to answer them."

"Good to know." Kenneth liked the sound of that and was sure he would take her up on the offer. Except for the fact that he was a notoriously slow reader and doubted she would be around much longer. "Why don't I get your number and give you mine, in case either of us have any further questions."

"Deal." Daphne grabbed his phone and punched in her number and then put his number in her phone. "There," she said, flashing a nice smile.

He couldn't resist smiling back. "Good luck with the research for your book. And enjoy the rest of your stay, no matter how long it may be."

"Mahalo." She chuckled cutely. "I have to get used to saying that."

"You will," he assured her.

"Hope so." Daphne laughed naturally. "When in Hawaii and all that."

He grinned, imagining her being in his native state for a long time. "Right."

"Well, I'll let you get back to work," she said. "I'm just over there in those villas, so I walked here."

Kenneth glanced in that direction, glad that she was close by and in one of the safest areas on the island in the Kaanapali resort. "Good," he told her. "Catch you later." He wondered if that opportunity would present itself. Maybe he should just ask her out and be done with it. She smiled at him and walked away while he admired the confidence in her stride.

Chapter Three

Honestly, Daphne felt as though she could have talked with the handsome police detective all day. Or at least she was comfortable enough with him that time seemed to almost stand still in his formidable presence. She had totally gotten Nelson out of her system and was amenable to becoming involved with someone new. Kenneth certainly seemed to hit the right marks as a person she could imagine having a romance with. Too bad he lived on Maui and she had made a comfortable life for herself in Tuscaloosa. Still, change could be good for you. Right?

Wrong, if it means not being entirely on the same wavelength, Daphne told herself as she sat in a swivel club chair on the lanai, enjoying the sights and sounds of Hawaii while sipping from a goblet of red wine. Been there, done that with nearly disastrous results. She was better off by herself if the alternative meant being in an unhealthy relationship. A long distance one didn't seem like a good idea, either. But what about a fling? Not really her thing.

Still, she imagined that Kenneth was a great kisser and probably an even better lover.

Let's not get ahead of ourselves, she thought, in spite of feeling warm at the notion while noticing wide-eyed as a gecko make its way across the floor. For all she knew, Kenneth was seeing someone right now. If so, she wasn't about to try and come between him and another woman. Hadn't cheating been the motivating factor for a jealous Norman Takahashi losing it and killing his pregnant wife and three others? That type of potentially deadly tripartite Daphne felt she would just as soon avoid, thank you.

But what if Kenneth were as free and available as she was? While pondering that, against the backdrop of her main mission on the island, Daphne also considered that he was in the middle of a new serial killer investigation that admittedly had her spooked a bit. It wasn't lost on her that she resembled the nice-looking females with long dark hair that the killer was apparently targeting. She had to watch her step, even while still determined to complete the research for her next book. Being paranoid was not a good mix for a true crime writer who was thorough in gathering the information she needed for her writing projects. Daphne cringed nevertheless when thinking about the woman who'd stalked her, Marissa Sheffield, in what turned out to be a dangerous obsession. Daphne had initially made the mistake of being genuinely flattered by what she had believed was simply an adoring fan. So maybe it wasn't such a bad thing after all to be a little paranoid while keeping a proper perspective.

When her cell phone rang, Daphne's heart did a little leap, thinking it was Kenneth missing her already. Instead, she saw that the caller was her editor, Gordon Yung. Mindful of the time difference between Hawaii and New York, she realized that it was 8:30 p.m., Eastern Daylight Time. Or past the point in the day when he would still be in his office. She accepted the video-chat request and Gordon's face appeared on the small screen. Asian American and in his mid-forties, he had short black hair in a French crop cut and sable eyes behind aviator eyeglass frames.

"Hey," he said in a friendly tone.

"Aloha," she told him, smiling.

"Hope I'm not catching you at a bad time while living it up in paradise?"

"You're not. I'm just sitting on the lanai of my villa, enjoying a glass of wine before heading out again."

"Good for you." He grinned. "Heard from the publicist that the signing was a big success."

"It was," Daphne concurred. "Everything I could have hoped for."

"Then it was worth it setting you up with the Maui bookstore."

"Definitely." She flashed her teeth and recalled her initial meeting with Ken, who turned out to be Detective Kenneth Kealoha.

"How's the research coming along for your next book?"

"It's coming," she told him. "I spoke with the lead detective in the investigation and got his input on the murder-suicide. He's made himself available if I need more info."

Gordon pushed up his glasses. "That's terrific. Looks like you're well on your way."

"Yes, I believe so." Daphne tasted the wine. "Have to interview a few more people and get some other basic data, then I'll head home." Somehow saying it made her wish this weren't so. Especially when she could see herself spending more time on Maui. Maybe with Kenneth beyond being a helpful detective.

"If you need to stay in Hawaii a bit longer for some R&R, then do so," he suggested. "Tuscaloosa will still be there when you get back."

"I'll keep that in mind." She smiled thoughtfully. "Beyond the research, rest and relaxation, I think I may already have the subject matter for my next book."

"Really?" Gordon peered at her with curiosity. "Do tell?"

Daphne told him about the serial killer on the loose known as the Maui Suffocation Killer and how this was in direct contrast to the idyllic beauty of the island.

"Sounds interesting, in an unfortunate way," he said.

"I think so, too. But it's too soon to know if this is what I should be looking at," she stressed.

"With your track record, if another serial killer story captures your fancy, I say go for it."

"Mahalo, Gordon." She welcomed his support, which seemed to always be there as she navigated her way from newbie to bestselling author in demand by the media and social media for what she brought to the table.

"Anytime."

After disconnecting the chat, Daphne finished the wine and did a little work on her laptop. Half an hour later, she hopped into her car and took the short drive to a gated community in Kahana, where she was allowed entrance, and pulled up to a Bali Craftsman-style two-story home on a cul-de-sac on Hua Nui Way. It was the house where Norman Takahashi perpetrated a mass murder-suicide. She got out and, using her cell phone, took a couple of pictures of the exterior, including the mature trees bordering the property.

She went onto the lanai porch and rang the bell. When the door opened, an elderly frail Hawaiian man with white hair in a comb-over style greeted her. "Aloha." His brown eyes crinkled at the corners.

"Aloha," she said.

"You must be the writer, Daphne Dockery."

"Yes." She gave him a thin smile. "And you're Ralph Takahashi?" she assumed, Norman Takahashi's father, who moved into the property a few months after the crime occurred.

"Yes. Come in."

Stepping inside, Daphne took a sweeping glance of the living room with its warm contemporary furnishings before turning back to its current owner. "Thank you for seeing me."

"No problem," Ralph said. "Can I get you a mocktail?"

She smiled. "That would be nice."

"Make yourself comfortable." He proffered a thin arm toward a leather chair.

As she sat down, Daphne pondered the events that would forever change the dynamics of the household. Ralph handed her the nonalcoholic drink with a mixture of fruit juices and said somberly, "This is where it happened..."

She saw the pain in his face and felt badly for forcing him to relive the memory, but believed it was important for readers to visualize the horrific incident. "I'm sorry for your loss," Daphne uttered sincerely, and couldn't help but think back to her parents' deaths.

"So am I." Ralph sat in an upholstered rocking chair. "But it happened and there's nothing that can change that." He paused. "But maybe your writing about it can help other families avoid what I've had to go through."

"I hope so." More than he realized. She asked him a few general questions about the day of the murder-suicide and if there had been any indications that his son would resort to such drastic measures.

"I knew Norman was having a difficult time

dealing with Jenny's betrayal, but I never thought he would take it that far. Ending her life was bad enough. But killing Sarah and Lucas in the prime of their lives and Donna, who was a good person, was unforgivable." Ralph sighed heavily. "I only wish Norman would have talked to me about what he was thinking of doing. Maybe I could've talked him out of it."

"People who commit these types of acts often tend to keep to themselves till the very last moment for fear of being talked out of it," Daphne hated to say, but believed. "Your son's sense of betrayal, right or wrong, clouded his judgment to everything else in his life at that moment. I doubt that you would have been able to stop him," she said, hoping to soften the blow of survivor's guilt.

"Perhaps you're right." He gazed out the window musingly. "Feel free to have a look around or take pictures, if you want, for the book."

"Mahalo." Daphne took him up on his offer and did so as quickly as possible before leaving. It wasn't till she was back on the road and returned to Kaanapali Beach for a casual stroll along the popular beach walkway that ran the length of the ocean side of the resort that Daphne had the distinct feeling she was being watched.

HE WATCHED HER like a hawk, but smartly kept his distance. It wouldn't do him any good if she spotted and recognized him, now would it? He slowed down as she slowed down. Picked up the pace when she did. She definitely intrigued him as much for her beauty and guts as her ability to write about people like him. Yes, she got him, even if she had no idea just how much. But soon she would find out what it felt like to be on the receiving end of a serial killer, instead of simply trashing them for a gluttonous audience, hungry for good reading material to detract from their own miserable lives.

Cozying up to the police detective in charge of the Maui Suffocation Killer investigation was a smart move on her part to gather information and maybe more. He supposed she intended to write a future book on the subject. Whatever her intentions—or the detective's, for that matter—it would not save her in the end. Like the others, she needed to be taught a lesson. A fatal one. But not yet. He still had time to work with before she tried to leave the island. From what he'd gathered in overhearing the two at the Seas Grill earlier, the true crime author was doing research on an incident last year where a guy killed his wife and others before taking his own pathetic life. This indicated she was staying put for the time being.

That was further supported by her going to talk with the old man, apparently in relation to the murder-suicide that took place at that house. He'd followed her there and back to Kaanapali, careful not to tip his hand, thereby taking away the element of surprise. When they met face-to-face, it would be on his terms, not hers. And certainly not when the detective was tagging along, who hadn't yet been able to figure out who he was or what he was up to. Not till it was too late for the author. As had been the case for the other victims who never saw him coming before he overwhelmed them and took their lives.

He pretended not to notice as Daphne Dockery moved away from the Kaanapali Beach walkway and headed toward the Kiki Shores villas. Having followed her there before, he knew what unit she was staying in. As such, no need to take any chances in pursuing her at the moment. Instead, he gave her no reason to be suspicious of him in particular as, while wearing sunglasses to hide his eyes, he continued to walk down the pathway, seemingly uninterested as she glanced back, as though expecting someone to come after her.

Not yet. All in good time. *See you soon, Daphne*, he thought, suppressing a laugh of amusement and confidence that she would soon be his for the taking.

THE SUFFOCATION SERIAL Killer Task Force meeting was held that afternoon in the Maui PD conference room. Kenneth was seated in a faux leather chair around the mahogany boat-shaped table as his boss, the Assistant Chief of Investigative Services Bureau, Martin Morrissey, spoke at the podium. Fifty years old and on his second marriage, he had only recently been promoted to the position. Under pressure from the Chief of Police, Wendy Kutsunai, to bring this case to a close, Morrissey pulled no punches in making it crystal clear that he expected real results, sooner than later. "Allowing the unsub to run rings around this department is not an option," he stressed, standing tall at six-five, with a sturdy build, steel blue eyes and shaved bald head. "One death under my watch is one too many. But ten women suffocated to death by some maniac is totally unacceptable. We all need to work harder to get this guy, before he kills again."

When Morrissey turned it over to Kenneth, he knew that there was no beating around the bush. They had screwed up in focusing on Zack Lawrence. Owning up to this was less of a problem than having to admit that they were no closer to nailing the real serial killer than after his first kill. At least it felt that way to Kenneth. In fact, they did have bits and pieces of information that gave them something to work with. But they needed to tie it all together in a meaningful way to identify the unsub and put an end to his reign of terror brought down on women in Maui.

Kenneth stood beside the large touch-screen monitor and, using a stylus, displayed the unsettling grotesque images of all ten victims, the clear plastic bags over their tortured faces. "These women all died needlessly at the hands of the so-called Maui Suffocation Killer as a result of asphyxia," Kenneth said painfully, "while being initially brought under the unsub's control by a stun gun." He proceeded to mention their names one by one out of respect and as a reminder that all were once attractive, vibrant human beings before their lives were extinguished by the fiendish killer. "Venus Delgado, a twenty-nine-year-old yoga instructor, Deena Moanalani, a thirty-year-old hula dancer, Yolanda Monaco, a twenty-three-year-old waitress, Tracy Lowndes, a thirty-four-year-old wife and mother, Harriet Zu-lueta, a twenty-eight-year-old actress, Nichole Ciminello, a twenty-two-year-old registered nurse, Gwynyth Johnston, a twenty-nine-year-old psychol-ogist, Luana Quesada, a twenty-seven-year-old real estate agent, Jena Sutcliffe, a thirty-three-year-old event planner, and Irene Ishibashi, a thirty-one-year-old fashion designer. All had visited bars or night-clubs the same night they were killed."

Kenneth switched to a single image, also with a plastic bag on her face. "Ruth Paquin, age thirty-one and an elementary school principal, is the only known survivor of the unsub. She was also attacked after being at a nightclub." He showed another pic-ture of her after recovery as an attractive, brown-eyed woman with long black hair worn in a wavy razored shag. "Due to her ordeal, Ms. Paquin had a brain injury and has only been able to give us lim-ited information on her attacker." Kenneth paused before putting on the monitor a photograph of their onetime chief suspect. "Zack Lawrence was once thought to be our unsub. Unfortunately, he fell off the radar when, aside from lack of hard evidence, Irene

Ishibashi's corpse was discovered at a time when Lawrence had been under surveillance."

Lastly, Kenneth put up a digital sketch of a thirty-something blue-eyed male with longish black hair in a textured crew cut. "This person may be Ishibashi's killer," he said in a hopeful tone. "According to the victim's elderly neighbor, Mary Cabanilla, a man resembling this digital image, courtesy of our forensic sketch artist Patricia Boudreau, was seen running from Ishibashi's residence. We can only assume that this person of interest may not only be responsible for Irene Ishibashi's death, but the murders of the other victims of a serial killer on the island—till proven otherwise. In other words, we need to identify the unsub in a hurry, and bring him in for questioning."

"We're working on that, even as we speak," Detective Vanessa Ringwald said matter-of-factly. "The forensic composite sketch has been released to the public in hopes we can identify the unsub."

"Good," Kenneth said, eyeing her still seated at the table. He understood that a sketch derived from the recollections of a woman pushing eighty, who admitted she was stressed out at the time, was still a long shot at best.

"Forensics is trying to see if any prints or DNA can give us something to go on in identifying a suspect in Ishibashi's murder," Detective Tad Newsome pointed out as he stood against a wall.

Kenneth nodded. "We'll see if they can come up with anything." Thus far, their serial killer had managed to avoid leaving behind any scientific evidence. Could that change?

FBI agents Noelle Kaniho and Kirk Guilfoyle added their thoughts to the discussion, with Noelle believing that, between their law enforcement agencies, it would not be long before a suspect was behind bars. Or as she put it, "He's running out of places to hide and we're never going to give him a moment's rest from looking over his shoulder."

Guilfoyle, a veteran of the Bureau, was more pragmatic, if not as determined to catch the serial killer. "We've been down this road before. Even with our best efforts, these types of crimes are not always solved overnight. Serial killers, by definition, are able to take two or more lives and get away with it on the short-term. And sometimes that turns into long-term. Can you say Trevor Henshall, Ted Bundy, Lonnie Franklin Jr., Gary Ridgway? Need I go on? Let's keep working together and get this bastard."

"Couldn't have said it any better myself," Kenneth stated with an edge to his voice. "Now comes the hard part, tracking him down before he can do more harm."

Morrissey gave Kenneth a stern look and said, "That's what I'm expecting of you and the task force. Bring the perp in and let the justice system do its job."

Kenneth gave him a respectful salute, but understood where he was coming from. It was all part of what was expected in his line of work. Either deliver or get out of the way and someone else would.

He had no intention of walking away anytime soon. Not unless there was a good reason for his doing so. Somehow, he ended up thinking of Daphne.

AFTER LEAVING THE police department, Kenneth got onto Highway 30 and headed home. He continued to think about the alluring true crime writer and fantasized about spending the night with her. Or even the day in bed, for that matter. But that was getting way ahead of himself, wasn't it? Maybe getting involved with someone who could be leaving the island any day now was a very bad idea. Maybe she was still caught up with her ex, Nelson Holloway. Kenneth didn't do well with rebound relationships. Not that he'd been involved in any romance in a serious way, as it turned out. If Daphne were to be willing to meet him halfway—wherever that was—then it could be a game changer of sorts.

The possibilities of romancing the writer waned in his head as Kenneth neared his house on South Lauhoe Place in Lahaina. It sat nestled on nearly three acres of land with great views of the ocean and Hawaiian islands of Molokai and Lanai. He'd purchased the single-story three-bedroom, two-bath plantation-style home two years ago, with investment savings and a small loan from his parents. Though he welcomed his little slice of island paradise and the privacy it afforded him from the rat race, Kenneth would gladly share what he had should the right person come along. Or was that asking too much?

He drove through the palm tree–lined driveway and reached the house. Inside, he walked across the engineered hardwood flooring, admiring the open floorplan that included floor-to-ceiling windows, a great room, gourmet kitchen and tropical ceiling fans in every room. He had outfitted it with an eclectic mix of vintage and contemporary furnishings. Front and back lanais offered him a spot to chill and enjoy the sights and sounds of his property that had a security system in place for further peace of mind.

After grabbing a beer from the stainless steel refrigerator, Kenneth flopped onto the armless sectional sofa. Barely noticing the gecko that scurried across the floor fearlessly, he picked up the copy of *The Accident Killer* from the bamboo coffee table, intending to read a couple of chapters at best. But the more he read, the more Kenneth found himself riveted. He wound up reading the entire thing and it gave him more insight into the dark mind of Oscar Preston and, by virtue, a greater sense of what they were up against in dealing with the Maui Suffocation Killer unsub.

Chapter Four

Daphne was already up bright and early when her cell phone rang. Seeing that the caller was Kenneth, she was eager to answer. "Hey," she uttered, tempering her enthusiasm.

"I read your entire book last night," he said flatly.

"Really?" This surprised her. Given his full-time duties in law enforcement, she had expected him to take his sweet time finishing the book.

"Yeah, I wasn't expecting that, either. But the truth is, I couldn't put it down. You did a terrific job, Daphne."

She reveled in his compliment. "Thanks."

"I have a couple more questions for you about it," he said. "I was hoping you could come over to my place for dinner tonight. I'd like to cook you a traditional Hawaiian meal before you leave the island, if you're game."

Daphne chuckled. "You cook?"

"Of course." Kenneth laughed. "Does that surprise you?"

"Not really," she lied. "Guess I'm just not used to men cooking for me."

"Maybe it's time to change that. So, are we on?"

"Yes, I'd love to experience a genuine Hawaiian meal while I have the chance," she agreed, unable to hide her excitement in dining with him and otherwise spend quality time. The fact that he could actually cook, which was not exactly her own strong suit when it came to anything extravagant, was another feather in his cap. "What time?"

"How about six?"

"Works for me."

"I live in Lahaina, so it won't be a problem to swing by and pick you up," Kenneth offered. "While letting the food work its magic."

Though it sounded appealing in an old-fashioned way, Daphne saw no reason to put him out. If he was doing the cooking, the least she could do was come to him. "I'll drive to your place. With a GPS navigator, it should be no problem getting there."

"All right," Kenneth said. "See you around six."

"Shall I bring wine?" Daphne wondered, feeling the need to contribute in some fashion.

"Not necessary. I have several varieties to choose from."

"Okay." She got his address and hung up, curious about how his investigation was going. As with her last book, she could only hope that the killer would be brought to his knees before he could hurt anyone else. *I'll ask Kenneth for an update tonight*, Daphne thought, as the notion of one day writing about the disturbing subject continued to intrigue her.

Gazing out the window at the inviting waters of the ocean, she decided to go for a swim before everyone else at the resort beat her to it. Minutes later, she had put on an orchid-colored one-piece swimsuit, grabbed a long towel and headed out. It didn't take long before she had walked across the sand, dropped the towel and dove into the water. Having excelled on the swim team in high school, Daphne immediately felt in her element as she started off with freestyle swimming and switched effortlessly into the breast-stroke and backstroke, before ending up where she began. She took measured breaths and felt the strain on her muscles while swimming through some ripples in the water. Even though there were no other swimmers in the vicinity and very few beachgoers, she felt a bit uneasy as though someone were spying on her.

Don't allow your imagination to run away with itself, Daphne chided herself. *No one's out to get you.* The one person who might have been was safely locked up in Tuscaloosa. And there was no reason to believe a serial killer had truly set his sights on her of all people. Was there?

By the time she had swam back to the shore, Daphne had chalked up her jumpiness to nothing more than misplaced paranoia just for the sake of it. After drying herself a bit with the towel, she padded across the sand and went back to the villa.

DAPHNE DROVE TO the Lahaina Banyan Court Park on the corner of Canal and Front Streets, where she had arranged to meet the sister of Jenny Takahashi, Katie Lacuesta. The park, which featured the largest banyan tree in the country, was near the Lahaina Harbor. After parking, Daphne approached a woman of medium build in her late forties with short gray hair in a choppy cut and hazel eyes.

"Katie?" Daphne asked to be sure.

"That's me," she responded with a tender smile.

"Daphne Dockery." They shook hands and Daphne thanked her for taking time away from her day to meet with her.

"I'm happy to help you get a more vivid picture of my sister," Katie expressed maudlinly.

They sat on a bench and, after getting permission to record the conversation, Daphne jumped right in. "Tell me a bit about Jenny?"

Katie's eyes lit. "She was a vivacious person, a great doctor and loving mother. Jenny never expected to fall out of love with Norman and in love with Francis, but it happened."

Daphne waited a beat before asking gingerly, "Did you know Jenny was pregnant before she was killed?"

"Yes," Katie responded equably. "We talked about everything that was happening in her life. Though the pregnancy was unexpected, she still looked forward to being a mother again and starting over with Francis."

"And he felt the same way as the *other man* in her life?" Daphne needed to ask.

"Very much so. He wanted to marry Jenny. They were in love. Francis embraced the idea of becoming a dad for the first time." Katie's voice broke. "To have this taken away by Norman out of spite was unconscionable. Just as it was to murder my niece, Sarah, and my mother, along with Sarah's boyfriend, Lucas. I hope Norman rots in hell."

Daphne gave her a moment while collecting her own thoughts. "Had Jenny expressed concern over telling Takahashi that she was leaving him?"

"Of course. But she never thought Norman would go that far in exacting revenge," Katie insisted. "Jenny would not have put her own needs ahead of the lives of those she loved. She would have stayed with Norman if it had come down to that, had she known he would commit a cowardly act of murder and suicide."

After a few more questions for clarity, Daphne ended the interview, knowing that Jenny Takahashi's spirit would live on in her sister and the coworkers she left behind. Including her erstwhile lover and father of her unborn child, Francis Hiraga.

Back at the villa, Daphne spent a few hours on her laptop doing research for her book, wanting to tell as complete a story as possible in presenting the truth to her readers.

When it was time to get ready for her dinner date, Daphne freshened up, brushed her hair and left it down, and changed into a floral-print midi dress and low-heeled slingback pumps. In spite of being a little nervous in what amounted to her first romantic-type outing with a man since breaking up with Nelson, she was more enthusiastic to see if it might lead to anything down the line. Or should she not look too far ahead when the time they could be together was getting shorter by the day?

The short drive down Highway 30 East, took her onto the Punakea Loop, and to South Lauhoe Place, where Daphne ended up at Kenneth's door. He was standing there, sporting a big grin and looking dapper in a yellow Oxford shirt, brown khaki pants and cognac-colored derby shoes. "Right on time," he said. "E komo mai. That means welcome."

She smiled while thinking that was a good step to feeling at home with him.

"You look nice," Kenneth said sincerely as he perused her.

"Thanks." Daphne flashed her teeth. "I could say the same about you."

"Mahalo." It was his turn to blush while knowing he wanted full well to make some kind of impression on her by cleaning himself up. "The food is just about ready."

"Smells delicious."

"It'll taste even better." He grinned at her confidently. "Feel free to look around while you wait."

"All right, I will," she said, taking him up on the offer with a warm smile.

On that note, Kenneth proceeded to head back into the kitchen, where he had prepared authentic cuisine he'd learned from his parents. That included Hawaiian green salad, mango-glazed baby back ribs, steamed white rice and sautéed mushrooms, and pono pie for dessert. He hoped he hadn't overdone it. That would be up to Daphne to decide.

"Your place is lovely," she gushed as he handed her a goblet of pineapple wine while they stood by the back lanai.

"Thanks. I like it," he had to admit while tasting his wine. But he also felt it lacked a woman's touch to truly make it a home. This made him curious about her place of residence. Would she ever be willing to leave it? "I'm sure you have a place that fits your needs."

Daphne sipped the wine, marveling at its taste, then said, "Yes, I'm happy with it." She paused. "Doesn't mean I couldn't be just as happy somewhere else, if it was meant to be."

Kenneth nodded musingly. "Yeah, I'm with you there." He wondered if he would truly be willing to leave the island. Yes, he loved it on Maui for all the right reasons. Still, if the right powers of persuasion were there, then why wouldn't he entertain relocating?

"Have you ever been to Alabama?" Daphne seemed to read his mind.

"Can't say that I have," he hated to admit.

"You should visit sometime. You don't know what you're missing."

Kenneth met her pretty eyes challengingly. "I think I have some idea."

"Oh, really?" Her eyes batted coquettishly. "What idea might that be?"

He pretended to think about it, enjoying this easy flowing banter between them. *I'll bite the bait*, he thought. "Let me put it this way, if you're representative of Tuscaloosa, then yes, I'm definitely missing something worth seeing."

Daphne flashed her teeth. "Good answer."

Kenneth laughed, but was dead serious. They would go down that road later. "Let's eat."

As they sat in wicker dining chairs around the rustic trestle gathering table and dug into the food, Daphne proclaimed, "It's delicious!"

"Mahalo." He couldn't help but grin, happy to cook for someone other than himself for a change. Even better would be to share the cooking duties. He imagined she could teach him a dish or two from her part of the country. And then some.

He watched as she scooped up white rice and said, "So, now that you've finished my book, what else would you like to know?"

Kenneth collected his thoughts while taking a bite of his salad. "First of all, let me just say again that I thoroughly enjoyed the book. Reads like a novel, but with all the twists and turns of a real-life crime story as it unfolds."

"That's the only way readers will connect without losing their attention," she contended.

"Makes sense." He stuck his fork into a mushroom. "How did you get Oscar Preston to grant you an interview? I assumed that most serial killers preferred to keep us guessing as to the nature of their criminal behavior."

"Actually, it's just the opposite," Daphne said. "The majority, if not all, serial killers are narcissists and only too happy to boast to the world about their killing ways and the ins and outs of it. Preston couldn't wait to tell his side of the story, no matter how disturbing and self-serving it was."

Kenneth frowned at the thought of the perp getting his kicks from bragging about committing multiple murders, but understood the value in the public knowing. "What took the authorities so long to figure out that the so-called accidental deaths were no accidents at all?" he asked curiously.

"Preston was smart enough to cover his tracks well for a period of time in that the deaths by accident and set far enough apart were plausible." She lifted a rib and took a bite. "But every ego-driven killer eventually becomes overconfident and slips up, as he did."

Kenneth thought about the Maui Suffocation Killer and wondered if he had slipped up as Daphne asked interestedly, "Any new developments with your local serial killer?"

"As a matter of fact, there has been a development," he answered, knowing that it had already been made public. "A digital sketch of a person of interest has been released. We're hopeful it's the break we've been looking for."

"Do those sketches really work in terms of giving a strong resemblance to the suspect?" she questioned, forking salad. "Or are they more likely to result in a flood of people claiming they know the person, even though they don't, throwing you off in the process?"

"The sketches aren't meant to replace a witness identification or photograph of a suspect," Kenneth pointed out. "Even if only reasonably accurate, it can be enough to get someone to recognize the person and lead to an arrest, no matter how many misses come with it. Of course, the sketches are only one tool in our arsenal in trying to nab criminals."

"I know that," she said ruefully. "Didn't mean to suggest otherwise. You guys have a difficult job to do and I can't imagine how the rest of us could ever rest comfortably if you weren't there to separate us from them."

"We all play our roles," he told her modestly, finishing off his rice and mushrooms. "I'm glad to be able to give it my all in getting the bad guys off the streets. Writing true crime books is every bit as important in the scheme of things to inform the public about what happens when we miss the signs all around us, emboldening criminals to continue to carry on as they see fit."

"I suppose." Daphne dabbed a napkin at the corners of her sexy mouth. "You're definitely good for my ego."

Kenneth laughed. "Just telling it as I see it." And he imagined there was much more to unravel in her appeal as a woman. "Hope you saved room for pono pie."

She smiled. "I think I can manage a bite or two."

"Good. So can I." He stood and began clearing the table.

"I can help," she insisted, getting up and grabbing used dishes.

Kenneth liked working in unison with her. He hoped they could put that to practice in other ways. Even if it wouldn't last. Half an hour later, they were out on the front lanai with their wineglasses and Kenneth felt compelled to say, "I have a confession to make."

"Uh-oh... Not sure I like the sound of that." Daphne looked at him warily. "You're married and you forgot to mention it before now? Or something even more unsettling?"

"No, not married. And no other dark secrets." He tasted the wine thoughtfully while meeting her eyes. "I did a little snooping about you. Or, more specifically, your relationship status. Saw that you broke up with Nelson Holloway." Kenneth wondered if he should have kept his mouth shut. "What can I say, I was curious about where things stood in your love life."

She sighed. "You could have just asked me. If so, I would have told you that Nelson and I ended things months ago."

"Sorry," Kenneth voiced shamefully. "Didn't mean to pry. Or maybe I did," he admitted, "but I should have just asked, as you say." He paused. "So, what happened between you two?"

Daphne sipped the wine. "Nelson was a jerk," she snapped. "And I was a fool for ever believing a word he said. End of story."

"That's good enough for me." Kenneth didn't want to push it any further for what was obviously a sore point for her. Still, again he wondered why Holloway would blow his chance with Daphne, something Kenneth could never imagine doing were they together.

"And what about you?" she asked curiously. "Why aren't you with someone?"

He considered the question before responding, "The short answer is I haven't met anyone I've clicked with to be in a steady relationship."

"What about the long answer?" she pressed.

Kenneth knew she expected nothing less than the truth. And he wanted to give it to her if there was to be any chance that something could develop between them. "I was once involved with someone. We started out as friends and seemed to be heading in the right direction toward something more serious. But then tragedy struck." He sucked in a deep breath.

"Cynthia, that friend, was killed and everything we hoped to have together died with her."

Daphne gazed at him. "She's the person you mentioned who was a victim of a serial killer in Honolulu?"

Kenneth nodded solemnly. "Yeah. Cynthia ended up being the last of ten victims Trevor Henshall murdered," he said resentfully. "Though I tried, there was nothing I could do to save her."

"I'm sorry you had to go through that." Daphne put a hand on his arm. "Nothing quite prepares you for that type of loss."

"You're right. It sucks, but it's just something you have to deal with."

"I know."

He held her gaze and understood that, in losing her parents to violence, she too had been put through the ringer and was also doing her best to live in the present while never forgetting what was unforgettable. "Anyway, that's my story. Doesn't mean I'm giving up on finding love that can last a lifetime, marriage, children, the whole bit."

"Neither am I," she told him, a softness in her inflection. "I want those things too someday."

Without judging whether or not this was something either could see in the other as a future partner, they found themselves sharing a tender kiss. Kenneth did not try to stop it, welcoming the taste of her soft lips on his, even while having no expectations. Nor did he pursue it further when Daphne pulled away and, just like that, it was over.

Chapter Five

"We've positively ID'd the suspect in the murder of Irene Ishibashi," Vanessa Ringwald said excitedly at the PD. "Name's Ben Hoffman, age thirty-six. Hoffman was one of Ishibashi's ex-boyfriends. He's currently unemployed."

Kenneth was not quite ready to pop open the champagne bottle just yet this morning. But he was certainly open to any news that indicated they could be closing in on a killer. "So the digital sketch did the trick in lining up with his real mug?"

"Yep, that and his fingerprints," she answered. "Dead giveaway."

Kenneth cocked a brow. "Explain?"

"I can do that," Tad Newsome pitched in. "Forensics was able to pull a print off the plastic bag over the victim's head, as well as another matching one from a sliding glass door at Ishibashi's house. They ran them through the system and came up with a hit for Hoffman. Obviously, he slipped up in his hurry to get in or out. Turns out, he's been arrested and served time for domestic violence and a DUI."

"Looks like we've caught a needed break," Kenneth said, not wanting to let this slide through their fingers.

"The sketch of the suspect was spot on." Vanessa pointed at her laptop screen. "Check this out. Here's Hoffman's mug shot and the digital sketch. Pretty much a dead ringer."

Kenneth was inclined to agree, crediting Mary Cabanilla for having a sharp eye in describing the man she saw leaving the scene of the crime. As well as Patricia Boudreau, their forensic sketch artist, for masterfully interpreting the description. "Let's get an arrest warrant and bring Hoffman in—the sooner the better," he stated, knowing that time was of the essence in capturing what could be the Maui Suffocation Killer.

"We're on it," Vanessa said, getting on her cell phone to get the ball rolling.

An hour later, Hoffman's black Volkswagen Tiguan was spotted on Halia Nakoa Street in Keopuolani Regional Park, with the driver matching the suspect's description. When police tried to pull the car over, Hoffman bolted. He led them on a high-speed chase to a residence on Kaikoo Place, where the suspect lived and was now barricading himself inside.

Wearing a ballistic vest and armed with a .40 caliber Glock 23 pistol, Kenneth sped to the scene, feeling they had a serial killer cornered and there was no way out for him, other than to surrender. Or be killed. His choice. The man had obviously decided against allowing the initial police he encountered to bring him in. Kenneth could only hope they could flush him out peacefully and interrogate him for some answers.

His mind drifted to the kiss between him and Daphne, which Kenneth could still feel on his lips. He had no idea what it meant, only that she had managed to stir something in him that he hadn't felt in a long time and he wanted to pursue it further. Assuming she was of the same mind. When he reached the location on Kaikoo Place, it was already flooded with cop cars and the Special Response Tactical Team was in place, awaiting further instructions.

Presenting his ID, Kenneth stepped inside the perimeter that had been set up around the two-story modern-style house, where neighbors had been evacuated as a safety precaution. Rendezvousing with other detectives and FBI agents behind a police van, Kenneth asked about the suspect, "Has Hoffman said anything?"

"Only that he won't come out," Newsome stated. "If you ask me, I think he's just posturing, hoping against hope that we'll back off."

"Yeah, right." Vanessa rolled her eyes. "Like that's going to happen."

Kenneth frowned. "Is anyone in the house?"

"It doesn't appear so," she answered. "According to one of Hoffman's neighbors, he lives alone."

"Let's hope that's true," Kenneth said. "Last thing we need is a hostage situation." Nevertheless, he didn't want to take any chances, ordering that a hostage and crisis negotiator be brought in to try and defuse the situation.

"I agree," Agent Noelle Kaniho said. "If Hoffman has anyone in there, he's desperate enough to try and use them as a shield to save his own neck."

"That's classic fugitive MO," Agent Kirk Guilfoyle argued. "But if he is alone in there, flushing out the suspect with all the means we have at our disposal shouldn't be much of a problem. That's assuming Hoffman wants to come out of this alive."

"One can only wonder," Kenneth said, when suddenly a shot rang out from the house, sending everyone ducking for cover with weapons drawn. Peeking behind the van, Kenneth could see movement from an upstairs window. The suspect apparently had no desire to end things peacefully. Another shot came from the house in Kenneth's direction, shattering a window in the van while forcing him to stay low to keep from being hit. "Everyone okay?" he asked nervously.

"Yeah, we're all still in one piece," Noelle said.

"Seems so," Vanessa concurred. "But barely. He's clearly out to get us before we can get him."

That appeared to be the case as more shots rang out, forcing the Special Response Tactical Team to return fire. There was no indication that the suspect had been hit, as he used the house for cover while peeking out the window but not standing directly in front of it.

"I'll try to talk him down," Kenneth said, not bothering to wait for the crisis negotiator. Or standing pat till the suspect had been shot dead. "I need a bullhorn." He was handed one and, while still crouching behind the van, spoke directly to the suspect. "Ben Hoffman, I'm Detective Kealoha, Maui PD. We need you to come out with your hands up. No one needs to get hurt. Least of all yourself. So far, none of us have been hit by your gunfire. Let's not change that. Otherwise, all bets are off."

"I'm not going back to jail!" Hoffman shouted. "Irene got what was coming to her. She refused to let me back into her life."

"What about the other women you killed?" Kenneth asked. "Did they deserve to die, too?"

Without giving an answer, a single shot was fired. Only this time it was within the house. Panicked, Kenneth tried talking to the suspect again. No response. There was a sinking feeling amongst them that Hoffman may have turned the gun on himself. But now was not the time to take any risks on their lives. "Let's give it a few more minutes and then we'll go in," Kenneth said, wanting to give them every opportunity to take the suspect into custody. Or lower the chance that he could still pose a threat, should they enter the house.

The hostage and crisis negotiator, a thirtysomething woman with short reddish-blond hair in an asymmetrical cut, arrived and attempted to pick up where Kenneth left off. "Mr. Hoffman, I'm Aiysha Nixon, a crisis negotiator. If you can hear me, please say something and we can try to negotiate your surrender."

When there was still no response, Kenneth could see the writing on the wall. "He's either seriously injured by a self-inflicted gunshot. Or dead. We need to find out either way."

Aiysha tried to speak to the suspect one last time, and when Hoffman did not or could not reply, she acquiesced to Kenneth and gave the go ahead to enter the premises. With the Special Response Tactical Team and armed detectives leading the way, a battering ram was used to force open the suspect's front door.

The house was in disarray as Kenneth went inside, equipped with a search warrant along with the arrest warrant. Scaling the carpeted stairs, he reached the second story and kept his firearm in readiness before entering the primary bedroom, where the suspect was unresponsive on the floor, apparently from a self-inflicted gunshot wound to the head. Next to him was what looked to be a 9-millimeter Luger semiautomatic handgun. There was no indication that the suspect had been wounded by law enforcement. But Ben Hoffman was still clinging to life.

Kenneth hoped he would pull through for all the

obvious reasons as the suspect was rushed to the
Maui Medical Center to try and save his life.

DAPHNE WAS STILL feeling giddy from kissing Kenneth
last night. Though it was something she wanted to
happen and was happy that it had, the timing seemed
off to go much further at that point in time. Still a
bit unsettled with the knowledge that a woman he'd
been so close to had been the victim of a serial killer,
the last thing Daphne wanted was to allow misplaced
feelings to cause either of them to do something they
might later regret. But if what she was starting to feel
for him was real and vice versa, she hoped the opportunity would still be there for them to delve into
the possibilities. Whether it was nothing more than
a fling in paradise or something that had much more
to offer for the long run.

She reached the Maui Medical Center on Mahalani Street and parked her car in the lot before heading inside. Doctor Francis Hiraga, the lover of Jenny
Takahashi, had agreed to speak with her. Daphne
was greeted by him in the busy lobby.

"Aloha," he said. "I'm Dr. Hiraga. Or you can
call me Francis."

Daphne debated this as she studied him. In his
early forties, he was around six feet and of slender
build, with black eyes and short raven hair worn in a
bowl cut. He had a three-day stubble beard and wore
a white lab coat over scrubs. "Nice to meet you, Francis," she decided, given the nature of their meeting.

He shook her hand and said, "I only have a few minutes to talk. Let's go to a room where we can have some privacy."

She followed him down a hall and into what looked to be a small lounge with a picture window. He sat in a gray tub chair and invited her to sit in the one beside it, after which Francis furrowed his brow and remarked sadly, "You know, I miss Jenny every single day."

"I'm sure you do," Daphne said sympathetically. "Losing someone like that is every person's worst nightmare."

Francis eyed her. "Sounds like you're speaking from experience?"

"Good observation." She told him about her parents' tragic deaths while getting his permission to tape the conversation.

"I'm sorry that happened to them," he said sincerely. "I have to say, though, that I never imagined in a million years that Norman Takahashi would do something so horrible as to take the lives of Jenny and our unborn child, their own daughter, Sarah, Jenny's mother and Sarah's boyfriend, Lucas. Then kill himself. It's just crazy. Why couldn't he have let Jenny go and moved on with his life?"

"That's something we'd all like to know." Daphne only wished she could get into Takahashi's head to try and understand why he and others like him felt such rage that a preference for death overcame the normal sanctity of life. "Did Jenny express any concern to you about leaving her husband?"

Francis scratched his pate. "Of course, it was of concern to her. But only because she didn't want to hurt him. The truth is she was worried more about how this would affect Sarah. Jenny didn't want her to be too confused and unsettled about being torn between two parents. But things hadn't been good between Jenny and Norman for a long time. She tried to ignore it, till she couldn't any longer."

Daphne reacted, remembering how things between her and Nelson had deteriorated over time and no amount of apologizing on his part could repair the damage. She was thankful that things had not escalated into violence between them. "How have you been holding up since the tragedy?" she asked the doctor poignantly.

"Truthfully, there's been good days and bad days," he said pensively. "I keep asking myself if there was something I could have done differently, short of never having fallen in love with Jenny and been given her love in return. I'd never want to take away the brief time we had together. She wouldn't have wanted me to."

"I believe you. I don't think she would have." Daphne looked at him and said understandingly, "As for what you could have done differently, we all tend to second-guess ourselves when things like this happen. In most instances, none of us can control what happens when people choose to do unpredictable or deviant things. We just move on with our lives as best as possible."

"I suppose you're right." Francis got to his feet. "Well, I have to get back to work. Never a dull moment around here."

"I can only imagine," she said, shutting off the recorder and standing. They stepped back into the hall. "Thanks for speaking with me. I know how difficult it was to do so."

"If you writing about it can bring some sort of closure to the ordeal of the past year, it was well worth it. Good luck with the book."

"Mahalo." Daphne smiled and was about to leave when she heard a commotion. She looked over her shoulder and saw a man being wheeled toward them on a gurney. There was blood coming from a hole at the side of his head, *undoubtedly from a bullet*, she thought, having seen this before as an investigative journalist.

"Code blue, Dr. Hiraga," she heard someone shout. "The patient has a self-inflicted gunshot wound to the head."

"You'll have to excuse me, Ms. Dockery," he said, his thick brows twitching with concern.

Daphne stepped aside, watching as he sprang into action, taking charge as the patient was moved hurriedly down the hall in an attempt to save his life. As she headed in the opposite direction, a bit shaken by the incident, Daphne found herself staring up into the face of Kenneth.

"WHAT ARE YOU doing here?" she asked him, trying to read into his eyes.

"I could ask you the same thing," Kenneth responded evenly, sensing that she wasn't seeking medical attention. A good thing.

"I came to talk to Francis Hiraga regarding his relationship with Jenny Takahashi."

"Oh, right." He should have guessed that, knowing that Hiraga was on staff and an important part of the story that ended in murder, mayhem and suicide. "How did it go?"

"As well as could be expected," Daphne said. "Losing the love of your life can be hard to overcome."

Even as she uttered the words, Kenneth could tell that she regretted saying them in recalling his own love loss. He wasn't quite ready to call Cynthia the love of his life, though, in spite of her early death. They were never given the opportunity to cross that threshold. Meaning such a love for him had yet to play out. "It's fine," he assured her.

Daphne nodded, then regarded him suspiciously. "You never told me what you were doing here." She glanced in the direction from which she had come and back. "The man who was just brought in…"

"His name's Ben Hoffman," Kenneth said tonelessly. "We were attempting to arrest him on suspicion for the murder of Irene Ishibashi when he holed himself up inside his house. Before the arrest warrant could be served, he shot himself. But not before trying to take out a few of us along the way. Fortunately, no one else was hurt."

"Thank goodness." Daphne breathed a sigh of relief to that effect and then a lightbulb seemed to go off in her head when she asked, "Are you saying that you think Hoffman is—"

Kenneth finished for her. "Yes, we have good reason to believe he may be our Maui Suffocation Killer..."

Before he could mention the DNA evidence and physical evidence indirectly linking Hoffman to the murders, Dr. Hiraga approached them, looking frazzled with fresh blood staining his lab coat. If he was surprised to see Kenneth and Daphne together, he didn't show it. "Detective Kealoha," he said with familiarity, no doubt from the investigation into the death of his married lover, Jenny Takahashi.

"Doctor," Kenneth acknowledged him.

"I understand you wanted an update on the condition of the patient brought in with head trauma from a gunshot?"

"That's right." Kenneth eyed him. "How is he?" Hopefully, they could keep the suspect alive at least long enough to question him, if not to be held accountable for his alleged crimes.

Francis shook his head. "I'm sorry to say that Ben Hoffman succumbed to his injuries. We did everything we could to save him. Unfortunately, it was not to be."

Kenneth had little choice but to accept that as he

nodded at the doctor and turned to Daphne, who also seemed to be digesting the news and its implications as it related to the terrorizing of women on Maui by the serial killer.

Chapter Six

"So, is the nightmare really over on the island?" Daphne asked later that evening.

They were at the Lahaina Second Friday Town Party in Campbell Park, right off Front Street. It was part of the Maui Friday Town Parties, where each Friday of the month one of five locations, starting with Wailuku and ending with Lanai, came alive with arts and crafts, live music and entertainment, and plenty of food choices. Basically, a big party with everyone invited. Kenneth thought it might be nice to show her another good side of island life to balance the not so good.

"One can only hope that's the case," he answered tactfully. The DNA found on the murder weapon—a plastic bag—that was responsible for the asphyxiation of Irene Ishibashi belonged to the dead suspect, Ben Hoffman. Similar plastic bags were confiscated from his home. A stun gun was also found among Hoffman's possessions that may have been used to subdue the victims. Open-and-shut case for him being the Maui Suffocation Killer? For some reason, Kenneth was not quite ready yet to make that call. It still troubled him that when given the opportunity after admitting to the murder of Irene Ishibashi, Hoffman chose to take himself out of the equation with a fatal shot to the head rather than confess to being the Maui Suffocation Killer. Was this a deliberate attempt to keep them forever guessing? Or was another killer still at large, waiting to strike again? "I'm guardedly optimistic we've got our man."

Daphne made a face. "That doesn't exactly sound convincing."

Kenneth was impressed at her ability to read him like a book. Maybe those instincts came with being a writer. Or this author, in particular. He flashed her an awkward grin. "I'm not totally convinced," he admitted truthfully, without elaborating. "Everything's pointing toward Hoffman as our killer. But it's in my nature to not jump the gun prematurely. Until we've fully cross-checked his history and the timing with the serial murders apart from Ishibashi's death, and wrapped up the forensic investigation in that regard, I'll stick with a guardedly optimistic approach that the nightmare on Maui has run its course."

She smiled. "Makes perfect sense. Guess that's what makes you a first-rate homicide detective."

He reacted modestly. "Not sure about the first-rate part, but I try not to leave any stones unturned for every investigation I'm involved in."

"That's a good way to look at it," she said. "Kind

of how I feel in writing true crime. There's no half stepping where it concerns making sure I've covered all the bases in telling the story."

"Based on the one book of yours that I've read," he told her with a grin, "there's definitely no half stepping in your style or substance." Kenneth realized that this applied to her as a woman as well. Something that kept him wanting to get in deeper with her as a man.

Daphne laughed. "Thanks. Now two-stepping is a different thing altogether. Though I can hold my own on the dance floor, I basically have two left feet."

"I doubt that," he said, picturing her as being a good fit in his arms in partner dancing. "I'd love to try the two-step with you sometime." No matter that he'd never done it before. He otherwise felt comfortable moving his feet on the dance floor.

"Hmm. If you're that courageous, then I'm in."

"Cool." He took that as a future date and fully intended to hold her to it while also looking beyond the dancing and to another activity they might be able to move their bodies in. "So, I guess hula dancing is out?" he joked, as they passed a stage that featured barefoot hula dancers strutting their stuff, alongside fire dancers, to the sounds of chanting and Hawaiian music.

"Uh, you probably guessed right." Daphne chuckled. "Looks like fun, though."

"I'll take that as a maybe," Kenneth said, believing she was as up to stepping outside her comfort zone in dancing as he was.

She wrinkled her nose. "Okay, I'll go along with the maybe."

As they continued to walk around, sampling food from vendors, Kenneth noted that Daphne suddenly seemed unsettled. "What is it?"

She grimaced while looking this way and that. "This may sound crazy, but I've had the strangest feeling that someone has been watching me."

His eyes narrowed. "When you say watching, do you mean as in stalking?"

"Yeah. I haven't actually seen anyone I could point out," she admitted. "It's just a feeling, maybe brought on after practically watching a serial killer breathe his final breaths before my very eyes. Probably shouldn't even have mentioned it."

"I'm glad you did," Kenneth told her sincerely. "I trust your feelings. Where there's smoke…" Maybe there was fire. Or something akin to it. He recalled that he'd joked about her stalking him when they met for the second time and she all but hit the panic button. Why? "Have you been stalked before?"

Daphne sighed. "Yes," she admitted. "Two months ago, an obsessed fan named Marissa Sheffield showed up at various signings and events in Tuscaloosa and elsewhere in and out of state. I didn't realize just how fanatical and dangerous until she demanded that I hire her as my assistant while insisting that we were bound to be best buds. When I tried to get her to back off, told her I didn't want an assistant or best friend, she became agitated and actually threatened me with bodily harm. It was really scary."

"I'm sure it was," Kenneth said, knowing this went well beyond your everyday adoring fans. "Where is she now?"

"In jail, charged with first-degree stalking, a Class C felony," Daphne replied with satisfaction. "At least she was when I left for my book tour."

"Hmm..." Kenneth wondered if her stalker was out on bail now. "Does she know you're in Hawaii?"

"I don't think so. Though my book tour schedule is public and easy to learn though my publisher's website, she would have no way of knowing I was planning to stay on Maui for a while, researching my next book."

"Maybe not." He scanned the park for any signs that they were being watched. No one stood out as being focused on Daphne. That didn't make him feel any more comfortable. Kenneth knew that any smart stalker would make it a point not to draw attention to him or herself. "I'll check on the status of Sheffield," he said. "In the meantime, if you still feel someone is following you, trust your instincts. If you see anyone who rubs you the wrong way, get a description of them and don't try to approach."

"I will and I won't," she promised to his last words of advice. Daphne touched him and said, "Thank you."

Kenneth again felt the heat of her fingers against his skin. It made him want to touch in return and experience even more of the sensations while hoping they were having the same effect on her. But he held back, as this was neither the time nor place to test the waters. Or maybe it was and he felt it was best not to go there just yet while they contemplated what they wanted or expected from one another. "Happy to do what I can to keep you safe while on Maui," he told her candidly. And in the process, Kenneth realized Daphne's safety and well-being was becoming important to him, wherever she happened to be. But especially in the face of danger. Perceived or real.

THE NEXT MORNING, Daphne went jogging on the walking trail, which meandered alongside the Kaanapali golf course. It reminded her of her favorite jogging path in Tuscaloosa and offered a beautiful view of the landscape up high and a perfect rainbow. She wondered if Kenneth was a jogger. Though they had not talked about his fitness routine, obviously he worked those muscles some way. She imagined them working out together, both in and out of bed. But would it ever happen? She could see them potentially in a serious relationship. Never mind the fact that they lived in two different places and hadn't progressed any further than a hot kiss and few sizzling touches. Those alone, however, had lit something in her that Daphne was sure he felt, too, and would need to be addressed one way or another before she had to leave.

With her hair tied in a low ponytail, she reached

the top of the hill and sucked in a deep breath while taking it all in. It was gorgeous, which she expected in visiting Maui. What she hadn't anticipated was having an actual serial killer at work in real time on the island during her visit, apart from the murder-suicide of the previous year that she was writing about. Thank goodness Kenneth and his colleagues had apparently put the brakes on the now infamous Maui Suffocation Killer. When the dust settled, she would certainly delve into it more deeply as she contemplated pursuing it as a true crime book.

For now, she had her plate full with the possibilities on both the personal and professional front up in the air. As she headed back downhill, Daphne instinctively looked over her shoulder, as if expecting a stalker to be hot on her trail. There was no one. *Guess I've been overdoing it in looking for something or someone that wasn't there*, she told herself. *Get a grip.* She decided to heed her own advice as Daphne continued to jog peacefully, giving an occasional wave to an early golfer or other runner.

When she arrived back at the villa, she went through a bottle of water and took a phone call from Gordon, her editor, who was checking up on her while fishing for her thoughts on the idea she put forth for her next book. "Heard that the Maui police had found their serial killer, who took his own life rather than be held accountable for his actions."

"So it seems," she told him. "The PD is still working on filling in the gaps before closing the case for good."

"I see," Gordon said. "And where do you stand on writing about it, once you've completed your current book? I don't mean to rush you or anything," he stressed. "There's plenty of time to decide where you go from here."

"It's fine." Daphne understood that he was just doing his job in wanting to keep the fires burning while the coals were hot. Who knew how long she would be writing narrative nonfiction crime stories before deciding to call it quits and focus on other things? Such as becoming a wife and mother. Not to say that she couldn't wear multiple hats at once, if need be. On the contrary, she was more than capable of continuing to be a writer and having a family. "I'm still contemplating the subject matter," she said honestly. "By the time I've wrapped up *A Maui Mass Murder*, I should have a much better idea of what my next project will be."

"Fair enough," he said acceptingly. "Hope you've taken some time to explore the island."

She smiled. "I have done some exploring and would like to do more before I head home." Of course, she could extend her stay, if need be, for one reason or another, including further exploration of Maui and all its wonders.

"Good for you. I hope to make it there one of these days myself. Think I'll try Oahu first, though, as I've heard so many good things about it."

"All are true," she assured him as Honolulu had been her first stop in Hawaii for the book tour. When another call came in from an unknown caller, Daphne cut the conversation short to take it out of curiosity. "Hello?"

"Hi," the female caller said nervously. "My name's Roxanne Sinclair. I was told that you're writing a book about the Takahashi murders and suicide on the island last year."

"Yes, I am." Daphne wondered how she got her number.

"I was having an affair with Norman Takahashi at the time," she claimed. "I thought he was in love with me. Then he finds out about Jenny being pregnant and in love with another man and goes berserk. If you're interested in what I have to say, we can meet for coffee."

Daphne was wary. Was this woman stalking her? Of course, she was interested in this unexpected twist to the story of Takahashi's life, if true. It would certainly add another element to the book. But what if it was fabricated in order to lure her into a trap?

"I'm not in this for money," Roxanne insisted, "or anything else. I just felt I was keeping this inside long enough and it needed to come out. But if you're not up for it, I understand."

"It's not that," Daphne told her, still with her guard up for some reason. "Do you have proof, like a photograph, that you and Takahashi were involved?"

"Yeah, sure." She made an indecipherable sound. "I just sent two pics to your phone."

Daphne pulled them up. They showed a man and woman in what could be described as being pretty cozy with one another. Daphne recognized the man as Norman Takahashi. He was slender, brown-eyed and had short gray-brown hair worn in an undercut style. Based on his appearance, it had to have been taken in his last year or two of life. She looked at the much younger African American female. In her early twenties, she was attractive with a light complexion and had long dark hair and big brown eyes. To Daphne, it was at the very least proof that Takahashi knew her.

"I have text messages between us," Roxanne said. "I can show you."

Knowing that she wanted the book to be as complete as possible, Daphne agreed to meet with her for coffee. What harm could there be in that?

An hour later, Daphne stepped inside the Coffees and Creams Café on Kaanapali Parkway in Whalers Village. She spotted a young woman who resembled the one in the pictures sitting at a corner table. "Roxanne?"

"Yes."

"I'm Daphne Dockery."

"Hi." She stood at around Daphne's height and build. Her long straight raven hair was loose with arched bangs. She was wearing a Hawaiian print T-shirt, frayed-hem denim shorts, and flip-flop sandals. "Thanks for meeting with me."

"You made it hard not to," Daphne had to admit. "I have to ask, though, where did you get my number?"

Roxanne did not flinch when she responded, "From school. I'm a student in the Mathematics Department at the University of Hawaii Maui College. You left your number there for Norman's successor, Professor Lynda Miyahira, whom I work for as a teaching assistant. Just as I did for Norman."

"I see." Daphne had, in fact, spoken briefly to Professor Miyahira by phone and planned to visit the college to get more background information on Takahashi. She smiled at his former student-lover. "Let's sit," she told her and both ordered cafe mochas and freshly baked pastries.

Roxanne nodded. "Okay."

There was small talk till their orders arrived and, with her voice recorder turned on, Daphne jumped right in. "So, how long were you seeing Professor Takahashi?" she asked inquiringly as she tasted her drink.

"For six months before his death," Roxanne answered matter-of-factly.

"He's quite a bit older than you."

"I know, but it didn't feel like it," she argued. "We just made a connection and were able to get past the age difference."

Daphne tried to imagine getting involved with one of her professors in college. She couldn't fathom it for all the right reasons. But what if he had been able to play on her vulnerabilities? Might she have found herself in a similar situation of awe, seduction and perhaps raging hormones? "Did Takahashi's wife, Jenny, know about your affair?"

Roxanne paused, her lower lip trembling. "Yeah. I told her, thinking it would help Norman to get past his reluctance to leave her." She sighed. "Guess I only made things worse. Two days later, he killed Jenny and himself, along with their daughter and the others…"

Daphne tried to come to grips with Takahashi refusing to accept his wife's betrayal and wish to leave the marriage, even while finding it perfectly acceptable to be engaged in an affair of his own. How selfish and outdated was that way of thinking? She suspected that Takahashi had cheated on his wife with other naive college girls. Perhaps Jenny had gotten wind of it before Roxanne, giving her license to pursue an affair of her own, falling in love with Francis Hiraga. Even if that were not true, she still had the right to want out of the marriage and Takahashi should have allowed her that much, whether he remained in a romantic relationship with Roxanne or not.

"Can I have a look at those text messages?" she asked her.

"Sure." Roxanne pulled them up on her cell phone and handed it to Daphne. She scanned them and read the explicit love and lust notes that made it clear that

Takahashi had been stringing her along into believing they had a future together.

Daphne handed her back the phone and asked bluntly, "Why would you want this exposed now, months after Norman Takahashi was dead and the relationship over? And how did the police not know about this in the course of their investigation?"

"Norman used burner phones when we communicated outside the office or bedroom, to try and hide the affair," she said. "Apparently, the police never figured it out. But now I need people to know there was another side to Norman than the one who went berserk." Roxanne wiped crumbs from her mouth. "He never laid a hand on me and was a good man deep down inside. He was just caught up between the past and a possible future with me and didn't know where to go with it."

Keep telling yourself that, Daphne mused sarcastically. Whatever decency Takahashi may have shown his young girlfriend, he threw it out the window where it concerned his own daughter, who wasn't much younger than Roxanne. Not to mention his pregnant wife, mother-in-law and another innocent victim. The carnage he'd left behind could not be easily swept under the rug. Even by someone who obviously cared deeply for him.

"I'll make sure that Norman Takahashi is given a fair shake insofar as the different sides of his character in writing the book," Daphne promised while remaining focused on its nature as a crimes-of-murder project. She took a final sip of her coffee.

"Mahalo." Roxanne seemed pleased with this. She stood and Daphne followed, the two shaking hands like old friends. "Good luck with your book."

"Thanks." She smiled at her as they walked out of the café and went their separate ways. Daphne contemplated the amazing twists and turns that always seemed to come with her profession. That included the serendipitous meeting of a certain homicide detective and any potential romance between them.

Chapter Seven

Martin Morrissey summoned Kenneth into his office for an update on the Maui Suffocation Killer investigation. Or more specifically, whether the death of Ben Hoffman meant the case had been effectively closed. Kenneth only wished he could say that were true. It would make things a whole lot easier for him and the other members of the investigative unit and task force. But he wasn't going to lead his boss astray by giving him a false read of the situation. Or jumping the gun in wrapping this up with a nice ribbon on top if he wasn't quite ready to go there yet.

Morrissey's brows twitched as he towered over his U-shaped gray desk, peering down at Kenneth seated in a stacking chair. "So, where are we in the investigation now that Hoffman is dead?"

"Better off than we were when he was alive," Kenneth said humorlessly. He knew that wouldn't cut it. "We believe that Hoffman is all but certainly responsible for the asphyxiation murder of Irene Ishibashi, based upon the DNA evidence and his own final words as a vindictive ex-boyfriend of the victim. Not to mention taking his own life rather than giving himself up. Ballistics was able to match the bullet removed from Hoffman's head to the shell casing and 9-millimeter Luger semiautomatic handgun found by his body, both with his fingerprints on them. All things considered, it stands to reason that given the MO, the presumption is that he also murdered nine other women. But I'm still not quite there yet to pin those on him."

"What's holding you back?" Morrissey demanded, pressing large hands on the desk.

Kenneth wanted to say a gut feeling, over and beyond the lack of evidence. *That won't fly*, he thought, instead saying frankly, "The timeline, for one. So far, we haven't been able to conclusively show through forensics or surveillance videos that Hoffman was present or in the vicinity at the time the murders occurred. This doesn't mean he wasn't. Only that it leaves open the door that he was a copycat killer. That's what we need to figure out before putting this case to rest. Officially."

"Well, get it done," he ordered, softening his hard stance. "The families of the victims deserve some real closure. That can't happen as long as this case continues to hang over us."

"I understand." Kenneth took this as his cue that the meeting was over. He stood, bringing them closer in height, making him feel less intimidated by the Investigative Services Bureau assistant chief. "We'll finish this," he promised while refusing to put a date and time on it.

After leaving the office and Morrissey, who had gotten on his cell phone to probably update the police chief, Kenneth was approached by Vanessa Ringwald. Her green eyes were wide with curiosity when she asked, "So, how did it go in there?"

"Just as you might expect." Kenneth took a breath. "Morrissey wants results that he can pass on to his boss and the families of the so-called Maui Suffocation Killer. I told him we'd deliver, but only when everything fits right to do so."

"Everyone wants this over," Vanessa contended. "With Hoffman out of the picture, we're clearly on the right track."

"We just have to be sure there's not more than one train to derail," he said wryly.

She nodded. "Yeah."

Kenneth thought about Daphne and her sense of being stalked. "I need you to check on the status of a woman named Marissa Sheffield. She was arrested for stalking Daphne Dockery in Tuscaloosa, Alabama."

Vanessa raised a brow. "Long ways from Maui."

"My thinking also," he said evenly. "Ms. Dockery seems to think someone may be following her around as she researches her next book on the island. If there's even a possibility…"

"Got it!" Vanessa smiled without further comment on his clear interest in the author beyond an official capacity other than to say, "I'll see what I can find out."

"Good." Kenneth rubbed his hands together. "In the meantime, I think I'll pay a visit to the only known survivor of the Maui Suffocation Killer, who may or may not have something to say about Ben Hoffman."

KENNETH DROVE DOWN South Puunene Avenue toward Wailea, a popular resort community in South Maui, where Ruth Paquin lived with her mother. Since her near-death experience with a serial killer, the grade school principal had been unable to return to work, still suffering from the brain injury caused by the attack. After turning onto Piilani Highway, he soon took a left on Wailea Alanui Drive and entered the Wailea Heights condominium complex, parking in the lot.

Passing by swaying palm trees and plumeria plants, Kenneth walked down a winding pathway to the ground floor unit and rang the bell. The door opened and a petite sixtysomething woman with ash-colored hair in stacked layers, whom he recognized from his previous visit as Ester Paquin, Ruth's mother, greeted him. "Detective Kealoha."

"Mrs. Paquin." He gave the widow a nod. "I was wondering if I could have a word with Ruth regarding the investigation into her attack?"

Ester reacted. "Yes, please come in." Kenneth stepped onto bamboo flooring in a small living room with rattan furniture. "I'll go get her," she told him. "Won't you sit down?"

"Mahalo." He sat on a wicker sofa while wondering if Ruth would be of any help to him in possibly identifying her assailant.

When Ruth entered the room alongside her mother, Kenneth thought she looked even frailer than the last time he saw the school principal. She had small brown eyes and her once long dark brown hair had been cut into a short messy style. "Aloha, Detective Kealoha," she spoke tentatively, then sat beside him.

"Hi, Ruth." He gave her a moment before asking gently, "How have you been?"

"I'm getting better," she said. "It's been an adjustment not being able to work, but my doctor tells me I'm responding well to treatment so I should be able to return to the school soon…"

"I'm happy to hear that," he said sincerely. "You probably have heard that a suspect in your case has been identified. His name is Ben Hoffman. He died from a self-inflicted gunshot injury."

"Yes, I saw the story on the news." Her chin dropped. "I was shocked."

Kenneth took a breath for what came next. "Here's the thing. We need to be certain that Hoffman was in fact the person who tried to kill you."

Ruth eyed her mother and back. "I don't understand?"

He took out his cell phone and pulled up Hoffman's

mug shot. "I need you to take a good look at this photo, Ruth," he told her. "To the best of your ability, does this look like the man who assaulted you?"

She studied the image for a long moment before saying, "My memory's still a little hazy, but seeing his face, it doesn't seem to be the same person who attacked me."

"Are you sure about that?" he pressed.

"I think so." Ruth's voice shook. "The attacker's face was rounder, eyes more closely set. Maybe it's all in my head, still playing tricks on me..."

Or not, Kenneth told himself. He wasn't sure just how much more reliable the witness was this time than before. Yet the mug shot didn't square with her initial description of the assailant, which she apparently maintained. In Kenneth's mind, this lent itself to the real possibility that they could be looking at two killers. One mimicking the killing method of the other.

Kenneth promised Ruth and her mother that he would keep them informed on any new developments in the case, even as he tried to keep an open mind himself on whether or not Ben Hoffman was actually their serial killer.

"HEY, JUST GOT news on your stalker, Marissa Sheffield," Kenneth spoke on a cell phone video chat.

"Oh..." Daphne tensed as she awaited what came next while sitting on a Louis XV armchair in her villa.

"Yeah, I'm afraid she was able to make bail," he said with a catch to his voice.

"Figured as much," Daphne muttered realistically, even if against her wishes. Should she be concerned?

Kenneth seemed to read her mind. "As far as we've been able to determine, she hasn't left the state of Alabama. Presumably, she'll stay put and won't bother you anymore."

"That's good to know," she said with a chuckle.

"Apart from that, do you know how to ride a horse?"

Daphne hadn't seen that abrupt detour coming. "Of course." She almost felt as though it went without saying. "When I was young, I rode horses every summer on my grandparents' ranch. Why do you ask?"

"An ex-cop friend of mine, Jared McDougall, who happens to be an expert in criminal background analysis, has a ranch Upcountry in Makawao," Kenneth told her. "I'm headed there to get some feedback from him on my current investigation and thought you might want to tag along. Since he worked on the Takahashi case, he can give you some insight on that as well, if interested. Jared usually likes to talk shop while riding one of his horses."

"Yes, I'd love to go with you," she said excitedly. "Haven't ridden in a while, but I'm sure that won't be a problem. I enjoy riding horses. I've also wanted to experience Upcountry Maui before I leave the island. It would certainly be a bonus to get Jared's take on Norman Takahashi."

"Great, then it's a date!" Kenneth's voice lifted an octave. "I can pick you up in half an hour."

"That sounds fine." Daphne looked forward to the adventure and liked the idea of it being a date, even if a working one. She gave him her unit number, but said she would meet him in front of the villas to save time.

"Be sure to dress accordingly," he teased her.

She laughed. "I will."

It was only after she got off the phone that Daphne began to wonder if she had anything to wear that was appropriate for horseback riding. Or would she need to go shopping with little time to spare? In going through her things, she settled on a pink short-sleeved sun shirt, boot-cut jeans and some comfort faux-leather boots she'd brought along. She put her hair in a high ponytail and applied suntan lotion and was ready to go.

With a little extra time on her hands, Daphne went to her laptop for a quick peek at info on Upcountry Maui. She saw that it was located on the western slopes of the Haleakala volcano and included the Haleakala National Park. Looking up Makawao, it was known as a paniolo town for Hawaiian cowboys and had a yearly Makawao Rodeo every Fourth of July. Seemed like a place she would love and imagined Kenneth as a cowboy, causing her to warm at the thought.

When Kenneth showed up on schedule, Daphne hopped inside the car. "Hey," he said, grinning at her.

"Hey." She smiled back, taking in his solid green polo shirt, jeans and paddock boots, while thinking that his attire more than measured up to her imagination. Including the Western felt black cowboy hat he wore. She chuckled. "You really are a cowboy at heart."

"Yeah, a little bit." He laughed and said, "Have something for you." Kenneth reached into the back seat and brought up a straw cowgirl hat, handing it to her. "Didn't want you to feel left out."

"How sweet." Daphne blushed and stuck it on her head, fitting perfectly. "Now I truly do feel the part. Mahalo!"

He grinned. "All set?"

"Yep," she said out of the corner of her mouth. "Let's go Upcountry."

During the drive on Highway 380, Daphne mentioned her unexpected sit down earlier with Norman Takahashi's girlfriend. "She had photos and text messages that backed up her story that they were having an affair."

"Wow," Kenneth said with surprise. "How did we miss that in the investigation?"

"Apparently, she kept this to herself until now," Daphne told him. "She wanted me to know so I could show a different side to Takahashi in the book, as someone she was in love with and claims loved her back."

Kenneth smirked. "Funny way for Takahashi to express this great love," he uttered sarcastically. "By leaving her wanting for someone who's no longer there. Never mind the hypocrisy of the jealous rage he exhibited in mass murder and suicide."

"I know." Daphne was in full agreement. "Takahashi was some piece of work."

"You're telling me." Kenneth made a grumbling sound. "My morning wasn't much better. Seems like the one survivor of the Maui Suffocation Killer, Ruth Paquin, doesn't believe that Ben Hoffman is the man who tried to kill her."

"Seriously?" Daphne's lower lip hung. "What does this mean?" she wondered.

"It means that either Paquin's judgment can be justifiably called into question," he replied, "or we could be dealing with a copycat killer. Meaning her would-be killer is still at large."

"That's a scary thought," Daphne had to say. Like everyone else, she had hoped that Hoffman's death would have spelled the end of the serial killer terrorizing dark-haired women on the island. What if this was a false assumption?

"Yeah, scary." Kenneth turned onto Piiholo Road. "I'm hoping Jared will have some thoughts about this to chew on."

"We'll see." She felt unsettled about where this investigation might be headed while at the same time wanting to see it through to its conclusion as a true crime story to possibly write about. Moreover, Daphne was happy to take this excursion with the detective as a way to spend as much time together as possible, with neither of them knowing where it was going.

JARED MCDOUGALL WAS ten years Kenneth's senior and someone he looked up to. After more than two decades in law enforcement, moving from the San Antonio Police Department to the Maui PD, he'd had enough. He chose an early retirement to buy a ranch, where he could raise horses, give riding lessons and offer scenic tours by horseback and trail rides. Though Kenneth didn't see himself calling it quits for the foreseeable future, he could see the day when he would hang it up and maybe get some prime property and more acreage of his own Upcountry to have a greater laidback life with a significant other he could start a family with. Someone like Daphne.

Jared was waiting outside when they drove up to his large Dutch colonial house on Waiahiwi Road. Single, he was the same height as Kenneth, but a thicker build and tanned from spending much of his time in the sun. When he was introduced to Daphne, in true cowboy style, Jared tilted the brim of his wool Western hat hiding curly gray-blond hair with a receding hairline, and aiming weathered gray eyes at her, said, "Read your last two books. Both kept me engrossed throughout."

"Thanks." She blushed. "I do my best to try and keep them real, yet readable."

"I can tell," he said. "So, you two ready to saddle up and we can talk?"

"Let's do it," Kenneth told him, and imagined how sexy Daphne would look on a horse.

"It'll be fun to ride and get a better appreciation of your land," she spoke eagerly.

Jared grinned. "Happy to show you around."

They went to the stables and Kenneth and Daphne came out with quarter horses and Jared a Clydesdale he'd named Grace after his mother. Kenneth would have happily helped Daphne climb atop the horse, only she did it on her own effortlessly and started riding as if she owned it, adding another layer to his fascination with her. She seemed just as taken with his own riding ability, which he'd also learned as a boy from his grandfather, who had a cattle ranch on Oahu. If Jared picked up the vibes between him and Daphne, he didn't let on, choosing to focus on their purpose for paying him a visit.

"Let's start with Norman Takahashi," Jared said as they rode down the trail surrounded by green grass, sloped land and koa trees. He faced Daphne, riding between the men. "I'm sure Kenneth told you I helped in the investigation."

"Yes, he mentioned that," she said. "I was hoping that with your expertise on criminal background analysis, you'd like to weigh in on what propelled Takahashi to take such drastic measures in murdering four people and killing himself." She threw in the new revelation that he'd been having an affair at the time.

"I'd be happy to shed some light on this," Jared said. "As far as the infidelity, I'd heard some whispers to that effect, but nothing that stuck. Kudos to you for getting Takahashi's mistress to come out of the woodwork with her story."

"I believe it was eating away at her and she felt this was the best way to find closure," Daphne indicated.

"She was probably right. Keeping things bottled up, no matter how difficult, is rarely a good thing." Jared took a breath and continued, "With respect to Norman Takahashi's willingness to end so many lives as a respected professor and father, in my view, he had a narcissistic personality that made him believe it was his way or no way. Moreover, I think he had a male-superiority complex that, in his mind, had Takahashi believing he had a right to do what he damn well pleased. But his wife, well...that was a different story. Especially with another man's child in the mix."

"Interesting," Daphne said, guiding her horse down the trail. "But why couldn't he simply have gone after his wife, if Takahashi couldn't bear to have her with another man? Why murder his daughter, her boyfriend and his mother-in-law for his wrath?"

"Good question," Jared said. "Of course, only Takahashi can answer that definitively, if he weren't in the grave. But based on my analysis of mass murder-suicide in general, the killer is usually trying to make a statement, albeit homicidal. Takahashi likely decided his actions were justified in taking out his rage on anyone who happened to be present when triggered to the point of no return."

"What about the mental-illness angle?" Kenneth asked curiously, knowing that such actions were typically thought of as the work of someone who was crazy.

Jared jutted his chin. "Only a small percentage of killers, whatever the type, suffer from mental illness," he pointed out. "The rest may try to justify their behavior because of the standard dynamics, such as anger, depression, jealousy, resentment or any combination thereof."

Daphne gave a little chuckle. "You really do know your stuff."

Jared laughed. "After reading your books, I could say the same for you."

She blushed. "Thanks."

"I agree with you both," Kenneth said admiringly as they picked up the pace. It was his turn to shift the conversation to the current serial killer case. He'd hoped they would have been able to close the investigation, but it still lingered in the air like the high humidity that characterized the island. He brought Jared up to date on what he hadn't already known. That included the lack of connecting DNA evidence between the killings and inconsistency with the presumption of Ben Hoffman as the Maui Suffocation Killer and the only surviving victim's belief that he didn't fit the description of the attacker still in her head.

Jared took a moment or two to collect his thoughts and said, "As you know, Kenneth, most serial killers are successful because they tend to leave few rock-solid clues, such as DNA and fingerprints at crime scenes for us to collect. So it's no surprise that it's not laid out in a neat package to point toward the perp definitively. That being said, serial killers make mistakes like everyone else. The fact that Hoffman's prints tied him to one murder could've just been sloppiness. Or indicative that his was only a single kill and a copycat killer, assuming Hoffman was even trying to confuse authorities. It may have been just happenstance that he used the same MO as the serial killer to murder his victim. I mean, there's only so many ways one can kill."

Kenneth lifted the brim of his hat. "Are you saying you think the serial killer is still out there?"

"Or could the surviving witness be off base with her reluctance to identify him as her attacker due to the brain trauma she suffered from the attack?" Daphne asked.

"You don't know what you don't know," Jared answered cryptically. "Obviously, if the serial killer never strikes again, one can make a strong case for Ben Hoffman as the culprit, given that the addictive nature of serial murder suggests that one will keep killing till caught or dead. Short of that," he said thoughtfully, "without having studied the extent of Ruth Paquin's brain injury, she may not have gotten a good enough look at her attacker to be able to identify him. But if I were to go with my gut instincts, I'd say that it's more likely than not that this thing may not be over with the death of Hoffman."

As Kenneth exchanged uneasy glances with Daphne while keeping the horse steady, his cell phone rang. He managed to take the phone out of his pocket, answering, "Kealoha." After listening to Detective Tad Newsome reveal some news, Kenneth told him levelly, "I'm on my way."

Daphne regarded his face as Kenneth stiffened. "What is it?"

"There's been another woman killed," he responded solemnly. "From the looks of it, with a plastic bag over the head and all, it appears that she was suffocated to death in the manner perfected by the Maui Suffocation Killer."

Chapter Eight

Kenneth would have preferred to drive Daphne back to her Kaanapali villa. But given that it was nearly twice the distance to get to from Makawao as the crime scene in Kihei, a bustling city in South Maui, going directly there was a no-brainer. Then there was also the fact that, sensing a story that fit into her wheelhouse as a potential true crime book with dramatic twists and turns, for better or worse, she had insisted on accompanying him as an interested observer. Or as she'd put it, "If this so-called Maui Suffocation Killer is truly still at it, alive and well, I'd like to be there to check it out for myself as a writer interested in island criminality in real time."

"How can I argue with that?" he'd said, knowing he was fighting a losing battle.

"You can't," Daphne told him determinedly. "I promise to stay out of your hair."

And I'd really love to run my fingers through your luscious long hair once it's down, Kenneth couldn't help but think in glancing at her ponytail while tempering his attraction to her. "Okay, you can come," he agreed. His only concern had been trying to protect her from the horrors of crime scenes. Or this one, in particular, that appeared to be the mark of a serial killer. Not that she needed his protection as someone who obviously was no stranger to immersing herself into crimes of violence as a top-notch researcher and writer. "Just keep away from the crime scene as a noncop, so as not to hurt the investigation," he warned and she agreed, accordingly,

Driving on Haliimaile Road, Kenneth soon came to Uwapo Road in North Kihei, where he swung right before entering the Kihei Creekside Apartments. After parking, they got out and he showed his ID to get them through the crime scene barrier.

"Remember not to touch anything," Kenneth said habitually, as they approached the building.

Daphne formed a tiny smile. "I'll keep my hands to myself."

He nodded, knowing that she would not be a problem. Entering the first-floor unit, where police activity was underway in securing, collecting and photographing evidence, they were met by Detectives Newsome and Ringwald in the open-concept living space, congested with traditional furnishings and people moving about on the travertine flooring.

Newsome glanced at Daphne, wrinkling his nose. "What's she doing here?"

Kenneth understood that Newsome's curiosity was probably getting the better of him, but her presence wasn't his call. Before he could respond, Vanessa said supportively, "What do you think? Ms. Dockery is probably here to research her next true crime book. Am I right?"

Daphne smiled thinly. "You could say that. At least I'm thinking about it. At the moment, I'm just an observer."

"Which I have no problem with," Kenneth made clear, peering at Newsome. "I've already advised her to not interfere as we do our jobs."

He backed down. "It's cool."

"Then let's get back to business," Vanessa said, "sad as it is and indicative of just what we didn't want to believe."

Kenneth shifted his gaze from her to Daphne and back again. "What do we have?" he asked characteristically, bracing himself for the gory details.

Vanessa frowned. "The victim, an African American female, age twenty-three, was found in the bathtub fully clothed. A plastic bag was left over her head, resembling that of the other victims of our serial killer."

"Including the murder of Irene Ishibashi," Newsome noted. "Only it's highly doubtful that the latest homicide was committed by Ben Hoffman, seeing that he's dead."

Unless it occurred before Hoffman took his own life, Kenneth thought, which admittedly was a long shot at best. He asked routinely, "And the name of the victim?"

"Roxanne Sinclair," Vanessa said, "according to her driver's license and student ID from the University of Hawaii Maui College."

Kenneth watched the color seem to drain from Daphne's face, prompting him to ask, "What is it?"

"I know her," she stammered. "Or at least we've met."

"When?" he asked.

"This morning." Daphne's voice quavered. "Roxanne was the student romantically involved with Norman Takahashi," she explained. "I can't believe she's dead."

Neither could Kenneth, considering. His brows drew together in assessing this. The timeline took Hoffman completely off the table as a suspect, while opening up new possibilities. Could Takahashi's murder-suicide be connected to a serial killer? Or were the two events totally separate and coincidental? Had Sinclair's killer been stalking Daphne and murdered the college student as a consolation prize?

"I want to see her," Daphne demanded.

"Probably not a good idea," Kenneth indicated, knowing how much it stuck with you seeing dead bodies, no matter how much one got used to it.

"Maybe it's a different woman," she suggested. "If not, since I was probably one of the last people to see Roxanne alive, we need to be sure it's her and go from there."

All things considered, her argument made sense, Kenneth knew. Even if he had little reason to believe

the driver's license and student identification ID'd
the wrong person. He agreed to allow Daphne without touching anything to see the victim while need-
ing to do the same himself.

They made their way inside the small bathroom
that had a separate tub from the step-in shower. A
quick glance by Kenneth at the granite countertop
showed the typical items such as an electric toothbrush, hair and facial products, and one used face-
cloth. His eyes locked in on the mirror above the
sink, where a red magic marker was used to write
the alarming words, *I'm Still Here. The Other Idiot
was a Copycat.*

Kenneth winced. If this was the work of the
Maui Suffocation Killer, had he targeted the victim at a nightspot and bided time before going after
her? Or had the unsub changed his m.o.? Kenneth
caught Daphne reading the disturbing message, before he homed in on the bathtub. The decedent was
seated in front of the faucet, wearing a print T-shirt,
denim shorts and was barefoot. Her twisted face,
surrounded by long and straight dark hair, was covered with a clear plastic bag, obfuscating her appearance somewhat, but still identifiable. Kenneth asked
Daphne, "Is this the same woman you met with this
morning?"

Looking at her with horrified eyes, she turned away
and uttered, "Yes, it's her—Roxanne Sinclair…"

Putting his arm around her, Kenneth said, "Let's
get you out of here." He led Daphne from the bath-

room, feeling her shaking at what she'd witnessed. "Sorry you had to see that." He tried to comfort her as they reached the living room area.

"I needed to," she insisted, pulling herself together. "Whoever murdered Roxanne may have been trying to send me a message."

"What kind of message?" Kenneth regarded her keenly. "Other than the one the unsub left on the bathroom mirror for us to find."

Daphne's face reddened. "The kind that says I'm watching you and may come after you next."

The thought of anything happening to her chilled him to the bone as Kenneth contemplated the notion of the two cases merging somewhat, even if on different levels. What if Daphne's sixth sense about being stalked was real? Only instead of a crazed fan, the stalker was a serial killer?

Vanessa weighed in. "Until we can get to the bottom of this, I suggest you watch your back, Daphne, if you plan to remain on the island for a while."

"I will," she promised, and eyed Kenneth. "The last thing I want is to be the target of a killer. But I won't be driven off like a scared rabbit, either. I have a job to do and intend to complete it."

"I understand," he said calmly while knowing he would need to do his part to keep her safe as long as she was on Maui. Even then, Kenneth was regretting the day when she would have to leave. But as long as she did so on her own two feet instead of in a casket, he would have to live with it. He motioned to Newsome and asked, "Who reported the crime?"

"No one we can identify," he said vaguely. "It was an anonymous call."

Which suggested to Kenneth that it came from the killer, who clearly wanted them to discover the body, along with this troubling message. "Let's see if we can trace the call," he said, knowing it was a long shot as the caller had likely used a burner phone.

Newsome nodded. "You got it."

Kenneth told him and Vanessa to double down on seeing if any of the victim's fellow tenants saw or heard anything as well as checking for surveillance videos. Someone had to know something, he reasoned while wondering if the unsub could actually be a resident at the apartment complex.

When Rudy Samudio, the medical examiner and coroner, arrived, he immediately went to do a preliminary examination of the decedent. Emerging, he had a dour look on his face as the decedent's body was bagged and carted away by his staff. "I thought this was behind us," Samudio groaned. "Apparently, I was mistaken."

"What's your initial take on the cause of death?" Kenneth asked him point-blank, sharing in his frustration.

"The decedent's death was all but certainly the result of suffocation," he answered without prelude, "caused by the plastic bag over her face, blocking the needed oxygen to the brain to survive." Samudio added, "Burn marks on her neck and arm are consistent with those made by a stun gun."

"Why am I not shocked?" Kenneth remarked sarcastically.

"Did you see the cryptic message the killer left on the bathroom mirror?" Newsome asked the coroner.

"How could I have missed it?" Samudio rolled his eyes. "Looks to me like you have two different killers—one dead and one very much alive."

"That seems to be the clear takeaway." Kenneth rubbed his jaw. "How long would you say this latest victim has been dead?" He needed to know, to be sure they were actually dealing with a second killer. Or the actual serial killer.

Samudio contemplated for a moment. "Pending a thorough examination, based on body temperature and other factors, I'd say that the deceased has been dead anywhere from two to four hours."

Kenneth could see a reaction from Daphne while validating in his own mind that Roxanne Sinclair couldn't possibly have been murdered by Ben Hoffman. It meant that the Maui Suffocation Killer was alive and well. Something they would have to deal with before the Suffocation Serial Killer Task Force could be officially disbanded.

"I'll take you back to the villa now," Kenneth told Daphne, believing that she had seen enough. As had he. But this was his job. She hadn't signed up for morbid crime scenes like this, even as a bestselling and coolheaded true crime writer.

HE STOOD AMONGST the bystanders outside the yellow crime scene tape, hidden in plain view as the police went about their work investigating the murder of Roxanne Sinclair. In spite of leaving them a message taking credit for killing her, while separating himself from the copycat killer Ben Hoffman, he wasn't about to turn himself in. Or confess right then and there to being the Maui Suffocation Killer. On the contrary, his work as a killer was far from over. Not when there were plenty of other women ripe for the picking, like perfect red apples. They needed to suffer as he had over his lifetime, getting little to no sympathy from anyone. Now was his time to shine and he gladly took on the challenge, daring anyone to try and stop him.

He watched as Daphne Dockery and Detective Kenneth Kealoha emerged from the building. Both looked weary. Or was it wary? He laughed within at the thought. The true crime writer had inspired him, making him want to go further than he'd ever thought possible in being a serial killer. Her books, especially the most recent one, had captured his fancy. She had, given him a whole new reason to try and outdo his predecessors as a hardhearted but clever serial killer. Roxanne Sinclair had been one example of that as an impromptu but necessary person to target for death. Before she realized the serious error of her ways in inviting him in, it was much too late to do anything but accept her fate as the next hapless victim of a bona fide killer.

Just as Daphne Dockery would soon be forced to do. She believed she was safe under the watchful eye of the detective, whose interest in the pretty true crime writer seemed to go beyond the call of duty. But he knew better. She would never be able to escape the trap he was setting for her, as long as she remained on the island. Even on the mainland, she could not rest easily, for he was just as capable of laying a hurt on her there from which she would never recover. Or be miraculously rescued by Detective Kealoha, as if she belonged to him. And only him.

No, the writer was his and it wouldn't be long before it was time to give her what she deserved. The type of oxygen-depriving death that the other women had suffered till their breathing stopped altogether. Then maybe someone else could write a book about famous true crime writers having the tables turned on them. He laughed again in his head while maintaining a calm and concerned facade for anyone who might look his way.

He watched as Daphne and the detective got into his vehicle, taking them away from the crime scene and its terror the murder had caused to spread around the apartment complex like a wildfire. But paradise came with a price. He would exact his revenge for being wronged while creating his own brand of pleasure for doing what he saw as right and ready to be carried out at the time and place of his choosing.

He effortlessly separated himself from the gathering, knowing he had gotten away with murder once again. It was time to chill and wait for the next person to die a cruel death. Until then, he would bask in his triumphs, knowing there was little that could be done to interfere with his actions. Which was unfortunate, as he had no plans to let up. Not when women like Daphne Dockery were out there, waiting to experience death, which he intended to deliver time and time again.

"I DON'T REALLY feel like going back to the villa yet," Daphne surprised herself by saying once they got inside the car. Or maybe the circumstances gave her the courage to put it out there and see what happened.

"You want to go for a drink?" Kenneth asked as they pulled onto the street. "I've got a little time to work with as the investigation unfolds."

"How about we go back to your place?" There, she said it. Would he take the bait and run with it? Or would duty call and need to be put on hold?

"We can do that." His tone was unreadable, but Daphne read his body language behind the wheel that told her they were very much on the same track. Or was that more wishful thinking on her part?

"Good," she said, leaving it at that while knowing she wanted him and had to believe he wanted her just as badly. In spite of the fact that they were both caught up in murder investigations that had mysteriously merged. And that her planned time on the island was coming to an end. It was certainly not long enough to think in terms of what sex might mean beyond being all hot and bothered for one night. But why give it a lot of thought, if he hadn't brought up? Just enjoy each other's company on a day they could both use a distraction.

Neither of them had much to say during the rest of the drive, even if Daphne's thoughts were filled, thinking about wanting him like she couldn't remember wanting someone. This was intermingled with concerns about whether or not she was being stalked by a serial killer and if she should be worried that her life could be in danger. Or was the murder of Roxanne Sinclair unrelated to the book she was writing and Daphne's presence on Maui?

When they arrived at the house, Kenneth asked, "Can I get you something to drink?"

"Beer would be nice," she said. Though not much of a beer drinker, Daphne had a taste for it at the moment.

"Beer, it is." He walked into the kitchen and grabbed two bottles from the refrigerator, opened them and handed her one in the great room while commenting, "It's been quite a day."

"That's for sure." She sipped the beer, gazing into his wondrous brown-gray eyes. "Do you think Roxanne was killed by the same man responsible for most of the other suffocation deaths? Or could he be the actual copycat killer?"

"Good question." Kenneth drank beer thoughtfully. "We'll have to see about that. If I had to make a call on this, I'd have to say that whoever murdered

Roxanne is the real deal, insofar as wearing the moniker, the Maui Suffocation Killer. He obviously went through great lengths to illustrate this, including the message on the mirror. Why Ben Hoffman decided to kill his ex-girlfriend, Irene Ishibashi, in the same manner, who knows? I can only assume that he was hoping to throw the authorities off. Might have worked, too, if not for the prints he left behind."

"Not to mention the apparent real killer seems determined not to let someone else take credit for his crimes," Daphne said, unnerved at the mental image of Roxanne in the bathtub with her face anguished from dying the way she had.

"Yeah, there is that," he conceded, locking eyes with her.

"Then there's this..." She tilted her face upward and kissed him, tasting the beer. The kiss lingered for a time before she pulled back and met his gaze. "In case you're wondering, I want you."

"I think that goes both ways." Kenneth's voice deepened. "Forget the *I think* part. I want you, too." He lifted her chin and they kissed again, this time with an even greater sense of urgency, as he slipped his tongue inside her mouth and she reciprocated. She could feel his erection straining to be released, deepening her yearning for him.

"Shall we go into your bedroom and continue this?" Daphne asked.

"Absolutely," he told her without hesitation.

"Do you have protection?" she thought to ask, taking another sip of the beer. Though the desire to be with him was overwhelming, Daphne knew it was wise to act responsibly for both of them at this stage of whatever was going on between them. Even so, she was sure he was good father material, should the day come that they were ever to go down that road in a relationship.

"Yes. Always." On that note, Kenneth took her hand and led the way into the bedroom.

Daphne glanced at the vintage oak furniture before narrowing her focus on the rustic panel bed, imagining them soon on it. Kenneth took their beer bottles and set them on the dresser before cupping her cheeks and resuming their kissing. Its intensity actually made Daphne feel lightheaded. All the more reason why she relished the thought of what was to come next.

Chapter Nine

Kenneth was beyond aroused as he watched Daphne strip naked, showing off her perfect body with full and firm breasts, small waist and shapely legs. She waited till last to undo her hair, shaking it into place as it cascaded down across her narrow shoulders. Seemingly just as enamored with his undressing, she laid atop the rustic tweed comforter and waited for him to join her. Grabbing the condom packet from the nightstand drawer, he tossed it on the bed, before commencing to what had been in his fantasy from practically the first time he laid eyes on the gorgeous author.

A sweet dream come true, Kenneth thought as he climbed onto the bed with the ceiling fan spinning overhead and kissed Daphne. She was tasty and tantalizing. *I could kiss her forever*, he mused, intoxicated by her scent. He forced himself to break away from the passionate kiss, wanting to pleasure her in other ways while resisting his need to be inside her. He kissed her chin and neck, moving down to her breasts, teasing her taut nipples with his lips and teeth, all the while running skillful fingers up and down her body, till settling between Daphne's legs, pleasuring her while she moaned softly.

Abruptly, she grabbed his hand to stop and uttered hoarsely, "I'd rather take that first journey together. Please…"

"I'd like that, too," he said, giving in to her wishes, more than happy to oblige as his own hunger for her threatened to explode. He put the condom on. Fitting himself perfectly between her moist thighs, Kenneth drove inside her, going deeper with each thrust as they kissed passionately and the sense of primordial needs enveloped them like a shroud, separating them from everything else in the sometimes dark and dangerous world at large.

He wasn't sure if she climaxed first or him, or if they reached that apex in unison, as Kenneth had been so caught up in the frenetic movement and harmonious moments between him and Daphne that he simply enjoyed the ride and was more than content to allow nature to take its course. It did, and then some. Only when they came out of it to catch their breaths, did their bodies stop trembling with satisfaction and their heartbeats slowly return to normal.

"Wow," was all he could think to say as Kenneth lay beside her, feeling the breeze from the ceiling fan cool them off.

Daphne giggled. "How about mind-blowing!"

"That works." He laughed. "It was definitely more than worth the wait."

"So, you were waiting for this?" she teased him.

"Yeah, assuming we ever reached that point, which I was in no way taking for granted," he assured her. "If so, I was sure it would be amazing."

"Glad to know you have good instincts." Daphne chuckled and ran her foot along his leg. "Guess we both do, leading to this moment."

"But hopefully not the last." Kenneth touched her leg draped over his, the creamy skin still damp from their sexcapade. He certainly didn't intend to put any pressure on her, knowing full well that she wasn't going to remain on the island forever. And with a serial killer still on the loose and possibly eyeing her as a victim, could he really blame Daphne for wanting to leave as soon as she could? Kenneth sought to moderate his words. "I think what I'm trying to say is that I like being with you, in bed and out. I don't have any expectations, but as long as you're around…"

"I get it," she said, "and I feel the same. I'm enjoying your company, too, for as long it lasts. No pressure either way."

"Agreed." Kenneth welcomed her words of encouragement, but was still pained by the thought of time running out for them to explore this further to see if it might lead to something much more significant than sex, meals, horseback riding and joining forces on the true crime front. Not to mention their paths spilling over into his current investigation. But none of that should detract from what had just happened and how good it made him feel. Should it?

I WONDER WHAT he's dreaming about? Daphne asked herself as they lay in bed in the middle of the night, with Kenneth cuddling her in his powerful arms. Hopefully her. And where this could go between them if they grew serious about each other and weren't frightened off by barriers such as long distance. And careers that might not always be in sync, even if they seemed to be a natural fit in many ways. *I'm not about to pressure him into something that he's not ready for,* she thought. Maybe she wasn't ready, either. Or maybe she was more than ready to be in a steady relationship again. Even get married and have two or three children. But only with someone who shared her vision of exactly what it meant to be committed to another person in body and spirit. Rather than like her ex who thought only about himself at her expense. Kenneth was different, Daphne knew. But that didn't mean they were meant to be together. Not yet, anyway. Right now, she just wanted to enjoy the intimacy that had thoroughly captivated her a few hours ago, giving them much-needed relief from the cases of murder swirling all around them like sharks in the water. Whatever either of them needed to do to stay ahead of the curve in their respective occupations, she was sure they would find a way. No matter the obstacles that came when dealing with people who liked to kill other people for one disconcerting reason or another.

When Kenneth began to stir, Daphne found herself aroused again and wanting more of him. Was he ready to go another round? Only this time without the sense of desperation that dictated their actions the first time together?

"You awake?" she whispered to him as if someone might overhear them.

"Yeah, I am now," he said sluggishly. "Can't sleep?"

"I can, but I'd rather not right now." Daphne was amazed at just how assertive she had become around him. Where had this come from?

"Hmm…" Kenneth kissed her shoulder. "Did you have something else in mind?"

She turned her head and kissed him on the mouth. "Yes, I do." She slipped a hand between his legs. "But only if you're up for it."

He chuckled. "I'm sure I can manage." After kissing her again, he lifted up and said, "Give me a moment."

Daphne waited for him to get another condom and come back to bed, whereby she took control, kissing and touching him all over while thrilling in the way his body reacted to this stimulation. He did the same to her, titillating her slowly and very surely, before she had worked herself into a frenzy. After putting on the protection, Daphne climbed atop Kenneth and guided herself onto him. He ran one hand through her hair and used the other to hold her hip firmly as she rode him like the quarter horse she'd ridden on his friend's ranch. Only Kenneth was decidedly all human male to corral. When she couldn't hold back any longer, she allowed herself to climb the mountain of sexual delight to the very top, and held his trembling body tightly as he joined her in sheer bliss. Afterward, all Daphne could think of was that she was falling in love with the handsome and sexy police detective, both scaring and beguiling her, before she fell asleep in his arms.

KENNETH ALMOST HATED to have to reconvene the Suffocation Serial Killer Task Force so soon after they had hoped it might be on its last legs, giving way to future task forces fighting crime on the island. He'd much rather be in bed, making love to Daphne as they had off and on last night. He hadn't been able to get enough of her. And she had made it clear that this worked in reverse as well, giving them both something to chew on. Instead, here he was, forced to come to grips with the reality that their serial killer investigation was apparently far from over and may have moved in a different direction with links to a mass killing on the island.

He swallowed, while standing at the podium in the conference room, and said, "I know we thought this task force had just about wrapped things up with the confirmed suicide of Ben Hoffman, thought to be the Maui Suffocation Killer. But new evidence has surfaced to indicate otherwise." Kenneth used the stylus to control visuals shown on the large touch-screen monitor. He brought up a split image of Hoffman and Irene Ishibashi. "While there's strong reason to believe that Ben Hoffman was responsible for the suffocation death of Irene Ishibashi in what appears to be a copycat killing, it's very likely that the actual serial killer is still out there…"

Kenneth put up a graphic image of the latest woman to die. "Yesterday, Roxanne Sinclair, age twenty-three, was found fully clothed in her bath-tub at an apartment in Kihei with a plastic bag over her face. According to the autopsy report, the vic-tim's death was caused by asphyxia, the same as ten other women on Maui over the last eight months or so. Only one of those can be accounted for with a suspect." He paused while switching to a picture of the note left on the mirror. "This message came from the purported killer of Sinclair, taking full credit for it while discrediting Ben Hoffman as being the real Maui Suffocation Killer. It's something we have to take seriously," Kenneth pointed out, "given that another young woman is dead and, with the esti-mated day and time of death, unless Hoffman has reemerged as a vampire, he's not our guy.

"Another possible twist to this sordid tale has emerged." Kenneth displayed side-by-side images of Norman Takahashi and Roxanne Sinclair. Paus-ing for a moment to collect his thoughts, he said with ambiguity, "According to Sinclair, she was the secret lover of Norman Takahashi who, last year, killed his pregnant wife, teenage daughter, her boyfriend and Takahashi's mother-in-law before shooting himself to death. Sinclair has provided photographs and text messages to true crime writer Daphne Dockery to support this claim. Now Sinclair is also dead, apparently at the hands of a serial killer, who appears to be changing his m.o., with no evidence that he and the victim ever crossed paths at a nightclub. Whether there is a direct connection between the cases or it's purely coincidental, it bears looking into as part of our overall investigation in solving the current case." What Kenneth left out of the equation for now was his fear that the still-active Maui Suffocation Killer may have set his sights on Daphne. As yet, she was the one person who was indirectly connected, through meeting with Roxanne Sinclair, to the Takahashi mass murder-suicide and the serial killings of now ten women on the island. Had the killer gone after Roxanne Sinclair in the course of stalking Daphne to muddy the waters somewhat in the investigation?

These were questions that Kenneth was determined to get to the bottom of while doing what he could to protect Daphne to the extent possible. As it was, there was only so much he could do at the moment. He didn't have the authority to assign a full-time detail to follow her around day and night. Nor was he able to stop Daphne from insisting on going back to the villa and continuing her own work in doing research for her next book. That was her right as a professional writer and bestselling author. Right now, his best bet for safeguarding Daphne was to try and solve the Maui Suffocation Killer case by IDing the unsub and getting the serial killer off the streets and behind bars, once and for all.

On that front, the task force was in full agreement. Kenneth listened as Agents Kirk Guilfoyle and No-elle Kaniho took turns in reiterating the Bureau's full support and resources in assisting them in the investigation. Detectives Tad Newsome and Vanessa Ringwald were, as always, on board in doing whatever it took to bring this case to a close. And though he would have preferred that Ben Hoffman was their man and no one else had to die, even Assistant Chief of Investigative Services Bureau, Martin Morrissey, recognized that, with Roxanne Sinclair's suffocation murder, a killer remained on the loose. Their job was to leave no stones unturned in pursuit of justice for her and the other victims of the Maui Suffocation Killer.

DAPHNE DROVE DOWN Maui Lani Parkway en route to the University of Hawaii Maui College, located in Kahului, where she was meeting up with Kenneth to speak with Lynda Miyahira. Roxanne Sinclair was a teaching assistant for the mathematics professor, who'd succeeded Norman Takahashi in the position. Aside from wanting to get some further insight on Takahashi, Daphne wondered if Professor Miyahira had any knowledge of Roxanne's life outside the school that might help lead to her killer. At least this was something Kenneth was interested in learning, with Roxanne being the latest victim of the Maui Suffocation Killer, who was no longer believed to be buried with Ben Hoffman.

I never thought I'd be drawn into this serial killer investigation, Daphne told herself. Certainly not before officially taking it on as her next true crime book. But the fact that Roxanne had been murdered just hours after interviewing her made the confluence all but impossible for Daphne to dismiss. Was she at all responsible for the young woman's death? Perhaps as a warning to not dig any deeper for the book? Or was something even more sinister at play here, with a serial killer deciding to bring her into his orbit, starting with going after Roxanne?

Quite naturally, Daphne was unsettled at the notion. As was Kenneth, who had questioned whether it was wise to continue doing research for her book as long as his case was ongoing. But facing danger was not new to Daphne. Hadn't she stood her ground when up against a stalker? And even found herself face-to-face with notorious serial killer Oscar Preston. Although he was shackled at the time, with a burly correctional officer in the room, it was still a dangerous environment for her in interviewing the killer. Though she surely did not court trouble, she understood that there was invariably a certain risk versus reward in writing true crime. Backing away from it now would only make her question her career choices later. She couldn't let a serial killer dictate the life she led. Any more than Kenneth could when he went into law enforcement and went about investigating crimes.

Daphne knew deep down inside that he understood this, in spite of natural reservations about her staying the course, the circumstances being as they were. How could he not? The fact that he respected what she did was one reason she was attracted to Kenneth. Another was their off-the-charts sexual chemistry, which brought them together in bed last night and gave her another reason for falling in love, aside from the physical attraction. He only wanted her to remain safe. Having him around was half the battle. The other half was seeing if there was more to look forward to between them.

She turned onto West Kaahumanu Avenue and made her way to the college's Mathematics Department, where Daphne found that Kenneth had beaten her there, waiting outside the professor's office. "Hey," he said, grinning slightly.

"Hey." She colored, thinking about the hours they had spent in bed last night, much of it awake with plenty of sexual action. "You could have gotten started without me."

"We're in this together," Kenneth reminded her. "Let's see what Professor Miyahira can tell us about Roxanne Sinclair and more."

"All right," Daphne agreed, and went inside the small office.

When seeing them enter, Lynda Miyahira stood up from her ergonomic desk. In her mid-thirties, she was small with short and layered brown hair with blond highlights and coal eyes behind square glasses. "Hello," she said nervously.

"Hi, I'm Daphne Dockery. Thanks for seeing us." She understood how difficult it must be.

"Detective Kealoha," Kenneth said somberly.

Lynda shook their hands and said, "I just can't believe Roxanne is gone. She was a great teaching assistant and a good student with her whole life ahead of her."

"I know," Daphne offered sympathetically, knowing no words could suffice.

"Please have a seat," she told them.

They sat in vinyl guest chairs and Lynda remained standing, leaning against her desk. Kenneth motioned for Daphne to take the lead, prompting her to say, "I met with Roxanne yesterday. She wanted to talk about her relationship with Norman Takahashi for the book I'm writing."

Lynda nodded to that effect. "Yes, I told her about your book and wanting to get some background information on Professor Takahashi," she voiced maudlinly.

"Roxanne said she'd been having an affair with the professor before he died," Daphne stated, wondering if she knew about it, having been in the department at the time.

Shock registered across Lynda's face. "What?"

She didn't know, Daphne mused instinctively. "Roxanne provided proof that it was going on. She was in love with him and believed, whether true or not, that he loved her as well."

"I don't know what to say." Lynda touched her glasses. "I had no idea that Professor Takahashi would get involved with his one of his students and teaching assistant. Roxanne certainly never divulged this to me, though I knew she took Norman's death pretty hard. I just thought it was due to what happened." She drew a sharp breath. "Now Roxanne's been murdered—"

Kenneth leaned forward. "This is where I come in," he said evenly. "We suspect she was the victim of a serial killer."

Lynda put a hand to her mouth. "Oh, no."

"Do you happen to know if Roxanne was seeing anyone recently?" he asked.

"We didn't talk much about her personal life. She pretty much kept to herself," Lynda insisted. "However, Roxanne seemed to be on friendly terms with another teaching assistant in the department. Joshua Winningham. I can't tell you anything more than that."

"It's a start," Kenneth said. "I need to get in touch with Winningham."

"I can give you his cell-phone number."

As she did just that, Daphne thought to ask, "Did

Roxanne ever indicate that someone was stalking or harassing her?" *That would be one way for a serial killer to target a victim before victimizing,* she thought.

"She never told me anything like that," Lynda said. "Maybe you could talk to some of the students in her classes. I can provide you her class schedule."

"That would be helpful," Kenneth told her.

Daphne eyed Lynda and asked curiously, "What can you tell me about Norman Takahashi when he was with the department? What type of professor was he?"

Lynda considered this. "Most people in the department liked Norman," she asserted. "He was approachable and truly seemed to care about his students and wanted them to excel in mathematics."

"Did he ever have any complaints about sexual harassment or other inappropriate behavior with students?" Daphne asked straightforwardly. "Or other staff, for that matter?"

She shook her head. "Not that I'm aware of. You can check with the director of the department, Doctor Mitzi Yamane. But from what you've told me, evidently Professor Takahashi had no boundaries for what he was willing to do and with whom. I'm only sorry that Roxanne had to be swept up in his troubled life."

"So am I." Daphne couldn't help but wonder if that extended after Takahashi's death, with Roxanne winding up in the crosshairs of a serial killer.

Chapter Ten

As fortune would have it, they were able to track down Joshua Winningham in an accounting class. Pulling him out in front of classmates might not have been the best thing to do, but with another woman murdered, Kenneth didn't have the luxury of cutting him some slack. Once they had Joshua in the hall, he studied him. The suspect was in his mid-twenties, tall and lanky, with a low fade brown-man bun and blue eyes. Flashing his identification, Kenneth said toughly, "Detective Kealoha, Maui PD, Criminal Investigation Division."

He was about to introduce Daphne, when Joshua gazed at her and stated, "You're Daphne Dockery, the true crime writer."

"Yes, I am," she acknowledged.

"I went to your book signing," he said. "Along with Roxanne."

"Really?" Daphne flashed Kenneth a thoughtful look.

"Yeah. We thought it would be fun." Joshua furrowed his brow. "I assume that's why you're here. You're investigating what happened to her, right?"

Kenneth wasn't sure if he was merely playing innocent along with being perceptive. Or what. "That's correct," he told him.

Joshua winced. "Murdered. I'm still trying to process this."

"I understand that you two were friends?"

Joshua leaned on one leg. "Yeah, we were." He shifted his weight to the other leg. "We hooked up a couple of times, but that was before she got involved with some older dude."

Kenneth knew that person to be Norman Takahashi. "What older dude?" he asked.

"She never said," Joshua claimed. "Had my suspicions, but it wasn't any of my business." His eyes widened. "You don't think I had anything to do with her death, do you?"

"That depends." Kenneth pursed his lips. "We have reason to believe that Roxanne was involved with Professor Norman Takahashi." He watched Joshua react as though he knew or suspected as much.

"Yeah, I thought so, too," he conceded. "Saw them hanging together from time to time, but she claimed it was just as his TA. Who was I to question it?"

"After Takahashi murdered his pregnant wife and others, then killed himself, do you know if Roxanne got involved with anyone else?" Daphne asked pointedly.

Joshua pinched his long nose. "If so, she never

mentioned it to me," he said. "But then again, it wasn't in her nature to talk about her relationships. If you know what I mean."

Daphne eyed him. "Would she have confided in you if she thought someone was stalking her?"

"Probably." His expression changed as if a thought had popped into his head. "Come to think of it, I did get this weird text from her yesterday. Didn't think anything of it till now."

"Do you have your phone?" Kenneth asked, assuming that was the case.

"Yeah." He took the cell phone out of his jeans pocket and brought up the text message. Kenneth read with Daphne. It said, I'm Still Here.

They exchanged looks as Kenneth remembered the disturbing message left on Roxanne's bathroom mirror that this mimicked in part. It apparently was sent by her killer, no doubt meant to double down on being the actual Maui Suffocation Killer instead of an imposter.

After Joshua produced an alibi for the time of Roxanne Sinclair's murder, he was allowed to return to his class with Kenneth reasonably convinced that he had nothing to do with her death.

DAPHNE FOLLOWED KENNETH to a place called Loraine's Grill on Hookele Street for lunch. After they were seated and ordered teriyaki glazed chicken to go with potato salad and fresh brewed coffee, Daphne had to ask, "If that text did come from Roxanne's murderer, what's he trying to prove? That he can play games with people's lives and get away with it?"

Kenneth sipped some water. "That seems to be the gist of it," he muttered. "Appears as though the unsub was counting on the text being discovered through Joshua Winningham's cell phone and the authorities being able to put two and two together in knowing that it was the calling card of the Maui Suffocation Killer. Or, in other words, it seems like the perp is intent on taking credit for the murders he committed, which now stands at ten, not count- ing the murder of Irene Ishibashi by Ben Hoffman."

"So, how will you be able to catch him?" she asked, as if the police hadn't encountered this type of thing enough to know how to use every method at their disposal to eventually trip up the perpetrator.

"By trying to outthink the killer," Kenneth said bluntly. "That is to say, working hard to figure out his next moves before he makes them. He obviously is enjoying taunting us and probably feels invincible. They all do, till they discover that's not the case and we either slap the cuffs on and haul them off to jail or they wind up dead themselves, one way or another."

Daphne grimaced. "In the meantime, young women like Roxanne Sinclair are left to take the brunt of the killer's rage."

"Unfortunately, it happens." Kenneth sighed. "More often than I care to admit. We can't read kill- ers' minds to stop them ahead of time. But we damn sure can do everything in our power to try and prevent as many deaths as possible."

"I know that," she told him, never doubting the seriousness in which he took this. Especially having lost a close friend to a serial killer. Writing true crime gave her an added perspective on how law enforcement was able to come together through adversity and track down some of the worst criminals, even if the process could be agonizing at times. She was sure that would be the eventual outcome in this instance, too. But until such time, women on Maui were still left to the whims of this psychopath.

Kenneth gave her an earnest look. "I don't want anything to happen to you."

Daphne took that to heart. "Trust me, I feel the same way. But there are no guarantees, are there?" she stated honestly. "No woman wants to see her life come to an end by a serial killer. We can only try to outlast them while living our lives." She realized it wasn't as simple as that no matter how many times she said it. The female victims in her book were proof of that.

"You're right," he spoke calmly. "You can't hide under a rock. Just do me a favor, don't let your guard down, even as you live that life. If something were to ever upend it…"

His voice broke and Daphne instinctively reached across the table to touch his hand. "Don't worry. I'm not a quitter," she promised him. "I have so much to live for." *You're one of those things*, she thought in spite of not knowing where they were headed.

Kenneth relaxed as he squeezed her fingers gently. "Okay."

HE FELT BETTER in listening to her speak with confidence, given the dangers poisoning the atmosphere. Still, as long as a killer remained at large, Kenneth knew he could not rest easily where it concerned Daphne. Though they hadn't known each other for very long, it was long enough for him to know that what he was beginning to feel for her was real and could be lasting, if things were to work out between them. If last night's torrid action in bed was any indication, that was a distinct possibility that he longed to explore further.

After the food arrived, he waited till they began to eat. Then, gazing at Daphne's face, Kenneth said, "About last night…"

She looked up from her plate. "Are we talking about anything in particular from last night?" she teased him.

"How about everything." He gave a half grin, aroused at the carnal thoughts, but resisted going further. "Let's just say, I enjoyed our time together."

"That's a relief." Daphne blushed. "For a moment there, I was starting to wonder."

"Don't," Kenneth made clear as he sliced into the teriyaki glazed chicken. "Just so you know, though,

I'm not a fling type of guy." He needed to put that out there for a reaction.

Her lashes fluttered. "And I'm not a fling kind of girl," she argued, sticking her fork into the potato salad.

"So, where is this going?" He angled his face while hoping this wasn't a mistake.

"You tell me." She drew a breath. "We live and work in different states, an ocean apart, Kenneth. I thought we both understood that going in?"

"I do understand," he confessed. How could he not? "That doesn't mean I have to like it."

"I don't like it, either," Daphne insisted. "But it is what it is. Why ruin a good thing by making a big deal out of something neither of us is willing to do anything about at the moment to change the status quo?"

Kenneth chewed some food and grudgingly admitted, "You're absolutely right. My bad. Shouldn't have mentioned it. I overstepped."

"I want you to feel free to say whatever's on your mind," she told him, sounding sincere.

"You, too," he said, still having regrets about causing friction between them. That was the last thing he wanted. Especially when there was enough pressure on them in their professional lives. And his own intent to keep her from falling into the clutches of a demented killer but still respecting Daphne's right to coexist on her own terms while visiting the island. *I can't blow it just because I'm falling hard*

*for her and can't stand the thought of this coming to
an end anytime soon, if ever,* Kenneth told himself.
But what choice did he have, other than giving in
to the reality that she had her life elsewhere and he
had his. End of story. He tried to pivot in a different
direction and smiled, causing his eyes to crinkle at
the corners. "Okay, how about we pretend I didn't
just put you on the spot and keep an open mind on
things between us?"

Daphne flashed her teeth. "Yes, an open mind
sounds great."

"Cool." Kenneth smiled again while already wondering if he could ever be satisfied with a short-term
involvement, even if more than a fling. Especially
when he knew deep down inside that he wanted to
be able to share a bed with her every night and do all
the things daily that couples did together. But was
this a bridge too far to cross?

THAT AFTERNOON, Daphne went jogging along the
Kaanapali Beach walkway, bypassing casual walk-
ers, while taking in the swaying palm trees and endless ocean with waves crashing against the shore. She
was still assessing her luncheon with Kenneth and
whether or not they were on the same page as far as
where things were headed between them. Yes, they
agreed that neither were into one-night stands as a
substitute for a real relationship. Yet, neither seemed
willing to commit to anything more. For her part,
she had no strong ties to keep her in Tuscaloosa. But

relocating to Hawaii to be with someone who had yet to clarify exactly what he felt for her, assuming it was more than sexual gratification, wasn't an option. She needed more from Kenneth if he expected more from her.

Am I asking too much of him? Daphne mused. Or should she settle for less than what she wanted in a man? She had so much to offer, beginning with all the love he could ever ask for. But she needed the same in return. Would she ever get that from him? She jogged through Whalers Village and ended up on Kaanapali Parkway lined with monkeypod trees. She ran down the sidewalk that bordered the resort hotels and condos, sidestepping a few geckos along the way.

Daphne thought about the murder of Roxanne Sinclair. What were the odds that someone connected to mass murderer Norman Takahashi would find herself a victim of a current serial killer? It seemed more than pure coincidence to Daphne. Yet, she found it a stretch to link the two directly, other than that Roxanne had a bad run of luck on both fronts. *The other connection between the two is me*, Daphne told herself as she crossed over to the golf course side of the street. Had her research on Takahashi played a role in his former lover's death? Daphne couldn't get herself to accept this. Especially given that she had never sought Roxanne out. Never even knew she existed until she was contacted by her.

No, whatever reason the serial killer had for targeting Roxanne, who fit the profile of the other victims of the Maui Suffocation Killer, he was solely responsible for her death. Daphne could only pray that the perpetrator was ultimately held accountable for his crimes. Just like Oscar Preston and the other killers she had written about.

As she ran up the hill on the sidewalk, Daphne took note of the man mowing the golf course fairway. She guessed him to be in his early thirties, on the lean side, with messy dark hair in a sideswept style. Though he was busy at work on the grass, his eyes seemed transfixed on her. *What's his problem?* she asked herself. Or was she only imagining him leering at her? She averted her gaze and continued past him, wanting to believe she had been spooked because of the latest events with a killer at large.

But when she turned around at the top of the hill and began her descent to return to her villa, Daphne saw that the man was now standing next to the mower, maybe ten feet from the sidewalk, as though waiting for her. He was wearing a uniform and his long arms were crossed as he gave her a menacing look. *Definitely not imagining his dislike for me*, she told herself as a chill coursed through her perspiring body.

Daphne wondered if he had been stalking her. How had she not noticed him before? Moreover, she couldn't help but wonder if he was also a serial killer, using the golf course as a convenient cover. She locked eyes with him and he broke into a laugh as if entirely amused. Or sending her a warning that he was onto her and coming after her. Impulsively, she whipped out her cell phone and took a quick picture.

"What do you think you're doing?" he demanded, clearly unnerved at the prospect of being photographed.

"I could ask you the same thing," she shot back. "Or is harassment part of your mowing duties?"

"Who's harassing who, lady?" His thick brows knitted. "Get the hell away from me, if you know what's good for you."

"I have a pretty good idea what isn't." Daphne didn't need to be told twice. She hightailed it away from the creepy guy, who continued to glare as she put some distance between them, but for some reason she still felt threatened.

KENNETH WAS AT his desk when he got the call from Daphne informing him that she was suspicious of a Kaanapali golf course groundskeeper. All things considered, he took her concerns seriously as she sent him the picture she took of the man. *He does look somewhat ominous*, Kenneth had to admit to himself. Could he have been stalking her? Or worse, be sizing her up for the kill?

"I'll check him out," Kenneth promised in the video chat.

"Thanks," Daphne said. "Maybe I'm freaking out for no reason. Or maybe there's every reason to."

He wanted to suggest she stay at his place for now,

but Kenneth had already been rebuffed before and didn't want to put any further pressure on her. "It was the right thing to have me look into the groundskeeper," he said. "Can't be too careful right now."

"You're right. No woman on the island can afford to be." Daphne made a face. "Certainly not the women fitting the profile of those attacked by a serial killer. That includes me."

"You'll be fine," Kenneth promised, forcing himself to offer a smile to that effect. "If you see him checking you out again, or anyone else who gives you cause for concern, let me know."

"I will." She smiled self-consciously. "Well, I have to get some work done. Catch you later."

"All right." He disconnected and wondered if that was an invitation to visit her tonight. Or vice versa? Either way, Kenneth knew that he didn't want what they had to end anytime soon. Wherever that happened to take them. He got on his laptop and looked up the Kaanapali golf course that Daphne described. Kenneth called and spoke to the course manager, Ricarte Ribucan.

After sending him the photo, Ribucan quickly identified the man as Matthew Hamilton, age thirty-four, who had worked for the golf course for two years and apparently given them no problems. When Kenneth did a criminal background check on him, he discovered that Hamilton had been arrested for making threats against a neighbor and being accused of stalking a coworker. Neither charge resulted in a conviction. In Kenneth's mind, that was still more than enough to haul him in for questioning.

Newsome volunteered to do the honors, picking up the person of interest without incident. "He tossed out a profanity or two, but wisely didn't do anything stupid," the detective told Kenneth as they looked at Hamilton through a one-way window.

"Whether he did anything stupid remains to be seen," Kenneth said. He headed into the interrogation room where the suspect was seated.

"What's this all about?" he demanded while running a hand through his hair.

Kenneth sat on a wooden chair in front of him, a metal table separating them. "You make a habit of intimidating women?"

Hamilton narrowed his eyes. "I don't know what you're talking about."

"We received a complaint from a Kaanapali jogger that you were harassing her," Kenneth accused him.

Hamilton muttered an expletive. "I say it was the other way around," he claimed.

Kenneth flashed him a warning look. "You'll have to do better than that. Unless you want to spend some time in police custody."

"Okay, I was checking her out. No harm in that."

Maybe not, Kenneth conceded. For the moment, he was more interested in what else the suspect may have been up to. "So you say," he told him tonelessly. "Problem is, stalking someone is a crime."

"I never stalked her—or anyone else," Hamilton spat. "If she told you that, she's lying."

Kenneth peered at him. "A woman was murdered yesterday in Kihei between five and nine p.m. Can you account for your whereabouts then?"

Hamilton shifted uncomfortably. "Yeah, I was hanging out with my buddies playing pool at Krista's Lounge on Lower Main Street in Wailuku. Ask any of them."

"We will," Kenneth assured him. Then he decided to see if Hamilton had an alibi for the times the other deaths occurred that were attributable to the Maui Suffocation Killer.

By the time he delivered the news to Daphne that evening at her villa, Kenneth had become convinced that Matthew Hamilton was no longer a suspect as a stalker or serial killer, but was still a jerk.

Daphne concurred on the last point. "Glad to know he checked out anyway as having an alibi in not being a serial killer."

"Yeah, that's true." Kenneth sipped the red wine he had brought along. "Better safe than sorry, though," he told her, not taking anything for granted where it concerned her health and well-being.

"Always," she agreed, tasting her wine. "Guess I sometimes read people wrong as far as their intentions."

"We can't be sure what Hamilton's intentions may have been if given the opportunity. He's been warned that if he even looks in your direction again…"

Daphne smiled at him, running a hand along Kenneth's jawline. "Thanks for having my back, seemingly time and time again."

"It's pretty easy to do," he admitted, kissing the inside of her hand. "Especially when your back is so soft and wonderful to touch. Not to mention the rest of you."

"Hmm…" She showed her teeth. "So you like touching me, do you?"

He grinned desirously. "More than I can say."

Daphne lifted her chin and kissed him. He tasted the wine from her lips. "You can always show me, to prove your point."

"It would be my pleasure." Kenneth kissed her this time, returning the favor, making sure it was a potent kiss that was a good start in the romantic business of touching and more. They went into the bedroom and resumed what he had started. After stripping off their clothing and putting on protection in the hope that they might end up in her sleigh bed, Kenneth made love to Daphne. He wanted to make sure she achieved every bit of pleasure he was capable of giving before his turn came to enjoy the total fulfillment he got from being with her.

When it was over and they were cuddling, Kenneth thought about telling Daphne that he might be falling in love with her. But he held back out of fear that coming after red-hot sex, the timing might not be right. Last thing he wanted was for her to believe it was his libido speaking rather than his heart. Instead, he was content for her to fall asleep in his arms, while Kenneth contemplated how she might take the news and where she stood with the future on the line.

Chapter Eleven

The following morning, Kenneth left Daphne sleeping as duty called. The Maui PD had received a request from the Portland, Oregon, Police Bureau to assist in the arrest of Rodney Okamoto, who had been charged with murder in a hit-and-run collision that left one teenage pedestrian dead and another critically injured. A tip led Portland authorities to believe that Okamoto, thirty-seven, had fled to the island, where he had relatives living in the resort area of Kapalua in West Maui.

It was close enough to Kaanapali that Kenneth agreed to join in on capturing the fugitive. Especially when he had been spotted entering a nearby store on Napilihau Street. Meeting up with Vanessa Ringwald and Tad Newsome in the parking lot, and members of the Maui PD's Crime Reduction Unit, Kenneth had already removed his duty handgun as he asked, "Is the suspect still inside?"

"Yeah," Newsome said. "Been in there about ten

minutes. Not sure what he's buying, but he's taking his sweet time doing so."

"Either that, or Okamoto knows we're onto him and is holed up inside with hostages," Vanessa said. "Aiysha's been called to the scene," she added of their hostage-and-crisis negotiator, Aiysha Nixon.

Kenneth nodded. "Good." The last thing they needed was a bloodbath, assuming the suspect was armed. Just as he was about to confer with the Crime Reduction Unit on contingency plans, the suspect emerged from the store holding a bag of items in his hand. He was short with a medium build and dark hair in a buzz cut. Without preface, Kenneth yelled out, "Rodney Okamoto, you're under arrest for a felony hit-and-run. Drop the bag."

Okamoto took a long moment to weigh his options, before doing the smart thing and obeying the order. "Okay, you got me." After setting the bag on the ground, he raised his hands, fell to his knees, and they converged. Kenneth was the first to reach the suspect, slapping on handcuffs and reading him his rights before handing him over to the Crime Reduction Unit for eventual extradition back to Oregon.

"Glad that ended well," Vanessa said, putting her sidearm back into its holster.

"Me, too," Kenneth told her, wishing that were true with all crimes they were tasked with investigating and apprehension of suspects. No such luck. It continued to weigh on him that the Maui Suffocation Killer remained at large and clearly had a thirst for killing that would likely not stop till they forced him to do so.

"I'm checking out some surveillance video near the Kihei Creekside Apartments," Newsome told him as if reading Kenneth's thoughts. "Hopefully, we'll see someone coming or going during the timeline of Roxanne Sinclair's death that will eventually lead to identifying the unsub."

"Let me know what you find," Kenneth spoke routinely while fearing that the culprit had more than likely been able to successfully execute his escape through tried and true methods that had worked thus far.

"Speaking of our unsub," Vanessa said, "I heard that the lone survivor, Ruth Paquin, has returned to work."

"Really?" Kenneth voiced with surprise, believing she would need more time to recover.

"Yeah. Guess her doctors felt she was ready. At least something good has come out of this."

"I agree," he said. "Getting on with her life is the best way to triumph over the type of adversity the unsub put her through."

As Kenneth headed back to his car, he got out his cell phone and called sketch artist, Patricia Boudreau. "Hey, can you meet me at the Manikiki Elementary School in Kihei and bring along your digital drawing tablet?"

"Sure," she answered. "Who will I be sketching?"

"The person who attacked and tried to kill Ruth

Paquin. I'm hoping, now that she's back at work, her memory is sharper and she can give us a better description of the unsub."

"Okay," Patricia said. "See you soon."

Disconnecting, Kenneth kept his fingers crossed that Ruth would be up to the challenge. He got in his car and called Daphne, wondering if she was up yet. "Hey," she said after two rings.

"Hey." He liked the sound of her sleepy and sexy voice. "Did I wake you?"

"No," she insisted. "Just enjoying my morning coffee and wishing you had hung around long enough to have breakfast together."

"I'll take a rain check on that." Kenneth welcomed the notion of having meals with her, day and night. "Had to respond to a fugitive-at-large call. It ended with no one getting hurt, excluding the teenagers the suspect mowed down in Portland."

"That's awful," Daphne moaned. "At least you're okay."

"Yeah." He was much more concerned about her safety, if the truth were told. But he appreciated the thought nonetheless. "Anyway, I'm on my way to see the lone survivor of the serial killer about putting out a new sketch of the unsub. She's apparently recovered enough from the victimization that I'm hoping she can do more to help us find the attacker."

"Good luck with that." Daphne made a sound from tasting her coffee. "I have exciting news of my own. My publisher has booked me to appear this afternoon on the *Aloha, Maui* television show to talk about my book."

"That's great," Kenneth said. "Congratulations."

"Thanks. Every little bit of promo counts, right?"

"Absolutely. I'll try to make it to the studio to check you out."

"Hope to see you," she said. "If not, you can catch it on TV."

"Okay." He hung up and started the car. Dating a gorgeous bestselling author in demand was something he was wrapping his mind around. Were they dating now? Or just enjoying each other's company till it was time to say goodbye?

When Kenneth arrived at the school on Lipoa Parkway, he was met in the parking lot by Patricia Boudreau. In her early thirties, she was tall and slender, with red locks in a pixie cut with an undercut at the nape of her neck and green eyes. "Hey," she said, smiling while clutching her drawing tablet.

"Let's see what we can get from Ms. Paquin," he said evenly. They headed to the front door and showed identifications before being let in and led to the principal's office. Ruth was seated at her L-shaped desk. Next to it was an areca palm plant. Kenneth smiled thinly and, after introducing her to Patricia, said, "Sorry to barge in on you like this, but when I heard you were back at work, I was hoping you could give us a better description of your attacker."

"I can certainly try, Detective Kealoha." Ruth

took off her cat eyeglasses. "Please have a seat." They sat in side chairs across the desk. "Heard about that poor young woman who was just murdered. How awful." She gave a weary sigh. "Will this ever end?"

"Yes, it will," Kenneth tried to assure her. "With your help, we'll catch him." He realized this was a tall order. But given that she had correctly rejected Ben Hoffman as the man who tried to kill her, giving them a better visual of the unsub could go a long way.

"I'll do my best," Ruth promised, pressing her hands together as if in prayer.

Patricia opened her tablet before saying gently, "Try to think back to when you first saw your assailant and what he looked like. Even the smallest details would be helpful. Take your time."

Ruth sat back in her faux leather swivel seat, closed her eyes for a long moment and said, "He seemed to be in his mid-thirties, was tall and had a medium build, I think."

"That's good," Patricia encouraged her. "What color was his hair?"

"Dark, maybe black or dark brown," Ruth responded.

"Long? Short?"

"Short."

"Curly? Straight?"

"I'm not sure," Ruth told her. "I think maybe it was short on the sides and fuller at the top."

"Okay." Patricia worked on the tablet. "What about his face?"

"Hmm… It was kind of an oblong face."

Patricia repeated the words as she drew. "What color were his eyes?"

"Dark brown, I believe," Ruth said, wringing her hands.

"Were they more close set? Or wide set?"

"I think wide set."

Patricia held the tablet up. "Like this?"

"Yes," she answered.

Kenneth wondered just how sharp her recollections were, given the brain trauma she suffered. Were buried memories able to be brought back to the surface over time?

"How about his nose?" the digital sketch artist asked. "Do you remember if it was long, short, crooked, fleshy, roundish?"

"I think it was fleshy and had a slight hump as if it had been broken," Ruth indicated. Patricia asked about the unsub's mouth and chin, and with the latter, if there was any facial hair. "Not that I can remember," she was told.

A few minutes later, Patricia said, "Tell me if this looks like the man who attacked you?" She slid the tablet across the desk.

Ruth put her glasses on and then picked up the tablet, studying the digital drawing. She put a hand to her mouth. "Yes, that's him…" She dropped the tablet as if it were a hot coal.

Lifting it, Patricia gazed at Kenneth and showed him the drawing, which he assessed. "Are you sure this is the man who attacked you?" he had to ask, knowing this was not an exact science, even for expert witnesses. And even harder for those victimized to give an accurate description.

"I think so." Ruth swallowed. "It all happened so fast, but that looks like the man in my head."

"Do you recall seeing him at the club you were at that night?" Kenneth asked.

Ruth stared at the thought. "I may have seen him there," she suggested. "If so, we never spoke. Not till he attacked me."

"What did he say to you then, if you can recall?" Kenneth pressed.

She sucked in a deep breath and her voice shook when answering, "You're going to die, like the others."

When they left the building, Kenneth regretted forcing the principal to relive the dark memories, but knew it was necessary to make the nightmares go away for her and the community in general. "Let's get this sketch out there as soon as possible," he told Patricia. "If this is indeed the unsub, we need the public's help in identifying him."

"I'm on it," she said. "Like Ruth Paquin, none of us females on the island can sleep very well at night while this bogeyman remains at large."

"I know." Kenneth gave her an understanding look and thought about Daphne as a temporary island resident. Unless he could change that, once this case was solved.

DAPHNE SAT ON the cream-colored couch on the set of *Aloha, Maui*, located on Hoohana Street in Kahului, with her hair tucked into a low chignon and wearing a yellow maxi shirtdress and dress sandals. Though she had been interviewed on live television more than once, she still managed to get butterflies, as if the entire world hung on her every word. Of course, she knew this wasn't true, but still wanted to make a good impression nevertheless in promoting the book. Beside her was the attractive host, Betsy Leimomi, slender and in her thirties with hazel eyes and long layered blond hair with cappuccino highlights.

When it came time for them to chat, Daphne readied herself mentally as Betsy said on cue, "Our first guest today is international bestselling true crime writer, Daphne Dockery. Welcome to *Aloha, Maui*, Daphne."

"Thanks for having me," she responded appropriately.

"So nice of you to come to our little island for your book tour," Betsy said sweetly. She held up a copy of *The Accident Killer*. "I've read this and, folks, it's a real page-turner. Why don't we jump right in, Daphne, and you can tell us a bit about the book?"

"I'd love to." Daphne showed her teeth. She gave a short summary of serial killer Oscar Preston and the horrific crimes he committed. Or just enough to whet the appetite. "The book chronicles his life of criminality, the victims' backstories, the system of justice at work, the trial, the verdict and so much more."

Betsy giggled. "Sounds fascinating. What other tidbits can you give us?"

Daphne picked out a few more points of interest before saying, "I'm afraid you'll have to read the book to find out the rest."

"Quite understandable," the host said. She lifted the book again. "Read this. For fans of true crime and gripping narrative nonfiction, I promise you won't regret it." The subject matter switched to Daphne's next book, for which Betsy said coolly, "I understand you're currently doing research on another frightening true crime, one that took place on Maui last year involving mathematics professor Norman Takahashi, who went ballistic and killed a bunch of people, himself included. What can you tell us about this for a sneak peek?"

Daphne outlined the basic premise of the mass murder and suicide that rocked the island, promising a chronicling of events that included adultery, betrayal, pregnancy, mass murder and the killing of oneself. She finished with, "There's a very good reason why the truth is described as more frightening and disbelieving than fiction. Stay tuned."

After the break, Daphne noticed Kenneth. How long had he been there? He sported a big grin, causing her heart to flutter. She hoped it wasn't evident to the host or audience. Otherwise, she might have to explain just how much her feelings had grown for the police detective. Before they had a chance to talk about it and how strong his feelings might be for her.

When the director signaled to Betsy it was time to talk again, she gazed at her guest and said, curiosity in her tone, "As you probably know by now, Daphne, we are currently being terrorized on Maui by a serial killer in our midst, referred to by some as the Maui Suffocation Killer. If you don't know, sorry to have to spring this on you as a visiting author hoping to catch some rays, sand and surf in between researching your next book."

Daphne gave a little laugh. "Yes, I am somewhat familiar with the serial homicides and the investigation," she admitted, glancing in Kenneth's direction, while mindful of sharing any sensitive information.

"Well, that's a relief." Betsy chuckled, feigning wiping her brow. "Now that we have that out of the way, as the author of a string of true crime bestsellers and clearly an expert on serial killers, in general, can you share some thoughts on the Maui Suffocation Killer? And whether or not you think that the authorities are doing enough to catch this guy and make it safe for us women to resume enjoying paradise, without the need to constantly look over our shoulders?"

Talk about being put on the spot, Daphne mused, regarding the second question. But she understood that it was the talk show host's job to push the envelope to keep viewers interested. That didn't mean she was about to step on any toes in the ongoing criminal investigation. Certainly not Kenneth's, as someone she knew was giving his all in trying to nab the perpetrator. Keeping her breathing measured, Daphne made eye contact with him and then faced Betsy, saying to her smoothly, "Regarding the serial killer on the loose on the island, all I can say is that, though it's rare in our society, some men and women do decide to kill people for various nonsensical reasons. I can only hope that this one is brought to justice as soon as possible, for all our sakes." She waited a beat for that to settle before taking on the other question squarely. "As for those investigating these crimes, I'm confident that they're doing everything possible to bring this case to a close. The Maui PD takes their job seriously, just as I take mine, and with any luck, they'll catch the killer before anyone else has to die."

"Couldn't have said it any better myself," Betsy claimed before giving the book one last plug and saying, "Mahalo, Daphne, for taking time out of your busy schedule to talk with us. We wish you all the best with your latest and future books."

"Mahalo," Daphne said dynamically, shaking her hand and walking off the set. Kenneth was waiting when she got to the back of the studio. "You came."

"Yeah." He gave her a broad smile. "You were amazing."

She cast him a doubtful look. "You sure you're not just saying that for my benefit?"

Kenneth laughed. "Positive. No need to embellish what everyone here believed as well. You killed it."

Daphne sensed that he had second thoughts about using those last three words as she pondered the serial killings that included Roxanne Sinclair as the latest victim.

Chapter Twelve

"I've seen that person before," Daphne said, studying the digital sketch of the suspect in the attack on Ruth Paquin.

"Really?" Kenneth looked at her as they stood on his lanai. "Where?"

"Hmm…" She seemed to strain her mind. "The book signing. Yes, he was there."

"Was he?" Kenneth voiced skeptically, given that the sketch was based on a description that Ruth could have been mistaken with after her attack.

"Yes," Daphne repeated, a firmness to her tone. "I'm almost positive that this is the same man I told you about who creeped me out at the signing with the weird way he was looking at me, like he had a disdain for me or something."

"As I recall, you said you couldn't describe him," Kenneth pointed out.

"I also said I would probably recognize the man if I saw him again," she countered. "Okay, this isn't an actual photograph of him or in a lineup, but it seems to be a pretty good representation, all things considered."

"Uh-huh," he said, going along with it.

She wrinkled her nose. "If Ruth Paquin and I share a mental image of the same man, don't you think it's worth looking into?"

Kenneth was warming up to the notion. "Maybe."

"I assume the bookstore keeps surveillance video. If so, they could still have video of the signing and a real image of the man in question, who just might be a serial killer when he's not reading true crime books."

"You're right." Kenneth couldn't argue with her logic. At the very least, if they were talking about the same man who attacked Ruth Paquin and presumably ten other women, seeing him on video could go a long way toward identifying him. "What do you say we head over to the bookstore?"

Daphne's face lit teasingly. "I thought you'd never ask."

They drove to the Aloha Land Bookstore and met with the manager, a fortysomething woman named Mireille Lacuesta with brown hair in an A-line cut. "Nice to see you again, Daphne," she expressed, her brown eyes brightening.

"You, too." Daphne smiled, then introduced Kenneth. "This is Detective Kealoha of the Maui PD's Criminal Investigation Division."

Mireille eyed him curiously, shaking his hand. "How can I help you?"

"We'd like to take a look at your surveillance video from Daphne's book signing, if you still have it."

"As a matter of fact, we do," she said. "We usually keep it for thirty-one days before taping over it. May I ask what you're looking for?"

"Not what but whom," Kenneth answered vaguely, adding, "We'll know when we see it, as part of an ongoing investigation."

"All right. Follow me."

They were led to a small windowless room that held the security system equipment. Mireille sat in a mesh chair at a corner desk and started searching through the video. "Let's see what we've got," she muttered.

"Stop there!" Daphne voiced after a short while and Kenneth realized he was looking at himself at the signing, causing him to blush. He wasn't sure the bookstore manager picked up on it. The thought of how far he and Daphne had come on a personal level since then moved him. He only wondered how far they could still go before whatever they had ran its course. "The man we're looking for would be before the elderly woman who should be just ahead."

"Okay. Tell me when," Mireille said, and backed up the video some more.

"There!" Daphne practically shouted as she froze the image. "That's him," she told Kenneth.

"You're sure?"

"Positive. I remember his clothes…and him," she insisted.

He asked Mireille to zoom in, which she did, allowing Kenneth to study the somewhat grainy image better. He could certainly see a resemblance between the medium-sized, dark-haired man who looked to be in his mid-thirties and the digital sketch. Moreover, if Kenneth weren't mistaken, he could swear that the unsub seemed to be making an attempt to avoid staring directly at the security camera, as though he knew precisely where it was located. *Why would he want to do that, if he didn't have anything to hide?* Kenneth asked himself. Perhaps there were more than a few skeletons in his closet.

"Can you go back a little more?" Daphne asked. Mireille rewound and was asked to stop. "Tommy."

Kenneth saw when the man in question handed Daphne his book. "Tommy?"

"That's the name he gave when asking me to write something in the book," she asserted. "It's come back to me."

"All right." Kenneth contemplated this, wondering if this was the unsub's real name and could be used to track him down.

"What's he done?" Mireille inquired. "Or shouldn't I ask?"

"You have a right to," Kenneth reasoned. "For now, he's simply a person of interest." There was no reason to tell her prematurely that they could be looking at the Maui Suffocation Killer paying her bookstore a visit. She didn't pry any further. "Can you make me a copy of this section of the video?"

"Of course," Mireille said.

"Beyond that, I'd like to take a look at your outside surveillance video from around the same time," he told her, hoping they might catch a break and get an even better image of the unsub on Front Street.

"Sure thing," she told him.

The outside video missed the suspect's face altogether, catching only the back of his head and clothing. Kenneth made a mental note to have detectives check the security footage of nearby shops.

"Can you check to see if this man used a credit card to pay for my book?" Daphne asked the manager. "Using the name Tommy, Tom or whatever?"

"I can try."

Kenneth considered this unlikely if this Tommy was their serial killer, since using a credit card could give away his identity. Something that the unsub had worked hard to conceal. But missteps did occur, even for killers and psychopaths.

As it turned out, Mireille was unable to narrow down the purchase of Daphne's title using some facsimile of Tommy to correspond with the timeline as a credit transaction, leading Kenneth to believe the man in question had likely paid for the copy of *The Accident Killer* in cash. But it still told him that the unsub had decided for whatever reason to buy a book about a serial killer and, at the same time, may have been using it as a means to surveil Daphne as a prelude to killing her.

"So, what happens now?" she asked outside the bookstore.

"First, I take you back to the villa," Kenneth responded equably. "Then we'll see if the video of the unsub can be enhanced even more so it can be circulated with motion and still shots, to go along with the digital sketch of the suspect. Hopefully, this will help lead us to a positive ID and we can bring him in for questioning."

Daphne nodded and frowned. "I hate to think that a serial killer was close enough to touch at the signing, but far enough away to stay hidden in plain sight."

"Maybe he overplayed his hand this time." Kenneth felt optimistic they had made a breakthrough that could pay off. "We'll see how it goes."

After walking her to the door, Kenneth gave Daphne a quick kiss, having wanted to do that all day but resisting the temptation, knowing that the more passionate they became, the harder it would be to ever let her go. Was it too selfish on his part to want her to remain on the island once her research was over and the danger that a killer had brought to Maui abated?

DAPHNE WORKED ON her laptop, trying to stay focused on finishing the preliminary investigation into anything and everything that played a role in the life and times of mass killer Norman Takahashi. It was such a tragedy, killing his pregnant wife and his own daugh-

ter, along with two others and himself. This brought
back fresh memories of losing her parents in a similar fashion. Never knowing what it was like to experience a normal life growing up had shaken Daphne
to the core and made her wonder if such would ever
be possible in a relationship and with a family of her
own. Her ex, Nelson Holloway, had only reinforced
her fears that she was doomed to remain on her own,
with no kids to look forward to doting over.

Then Kenneth had entered her life and given
Daphne reason to believe that what they had was
real. It certainly felt that way. At least for her. But
though he had intimated strong feelings for her, until
he was more direct on where things stood between
them, she couldn't put her life on hold. Or risk having
her heart broken on sexual chemistry and promising
possibilities alone. *I can't put myself through such
disappointment again*, Daphne mused as she refo-
cused on prepping for her next book. And weighing
on her mind nearly as much was the ongoing serial
killer investigation on the island that she had unwittingly become a part of. First, with the murder
of Takahashi's lover, Roxanne Sinclair, believed to
be by the killer. And now, with the real likelihood
that the unsub had brazenly come to her book signing, potentially posing a real danger to her should he
remain on the loose. But running away from Maui
before things were resolved one way or the other between her and Kenneth wasn't something Daphne
was prepared to do. Was this a wise decision?

When a knock on the door was followed by the loud words, "Housekeeping," startling Daphne, she put the laptop to sleep and padded from the room in her bare feet, knowing that she did need some fresh towels. The moment she opened the door, having never bothered to look through the peephole, Daphne regretted it. Standing there was someone she thought she would never see again.

Marissa Sheffield looked like her. At least at a glance. She was attractive at twenty-seven, five years younger than Daphne, but the same height and slender build. She had the same heart-shaped face and bold blue eyes that could have passed for blue-green. Her once long and layered black hair had been cut, perhaps to make it harder to track her, and was now in an unruly inverted bob style. She was dressed in a sleeveless beige tank top with tapered boyfriend jeans and white sneakers.

Her wide mouth cracked an amused one-sided grin. "I can see you're surprised to see me, Daphne."

That was an understatement, to say the least. Forcing words to her mouth, Daphne's voice trembled when she said, "How did you find me?"

Before Daphne could react to prevent it, her stalker had barreled her way into the villa, almost daring Daphne to get in her way. Though her first instinct was to run as far as she could while screaming for help, curiosity got the better of Daphne as she went inside, though keeping her distance.

Marissa looked around and marveled, "Hey, this is really nice."

Daphne narrowed her eyes. "Are you going to answer me, or what?"

"Sure." Marissa flopped onto a leather suede armchair. "To tell you the truth, it wasn't all that difficult. On your website, you were only too happy to talk about your book tour in Hawaii that ended on Maui. Then I picked up bits and pieces on your new book deal and plans to write about a murder-suicide that took place on the island. I put two and two together to figure out that you were still here, waiting for me to find you." She giggled like a teenage girl. "Voilà, here I am."

Daphne frowned. "How long have you been on the island?" she asked, remembering the feeling of being followed.

"Long enough," Marissa responded vaguely. "All that matters is this is where I'm supposed to be, with you."

You're sick, Daphne told herself, but didn't dare say it out loud at risk of ticking her off. Who knew what her stalker was capable of? "You have to leave, okay?" Her voice was measured but with resolve. "I'm here for work, not play."

Marissa regarded her unaffectedly. "I can help you. As your personal assistant, remember? Just tell me what you need."

Daphne ventured a step closer. *Maybe if I'm straight with her, this can end peacefully*, she thought.

"What I need is for you to leave me alone, Marissa. I thought I'd made myself perfectly clear in Tuscaloosa. I don't need an assistant or friend. I'm hoping you'll respect that and go away. If you do, I won't call the police and report you for stalking me again."

Marissa shot to her feet, scowling, causing Daphne to take an involuntary step backward. "I'm not going back to jail. It was awful in there. If you try to put me there again, you'll be sorry."

I'm already sorry for letting down my guard, Daphne told herself. But she had to stand her ground. Otherwise, she might never be rid of her. Especially since the authorities weren't able to hold onto her. "You don't have to go to jail, Marissa," she spoke softly. "But I think you do need help. Following someone around against her wishes is not cool. I get that you like my writing and all, but this has got to stop."

"No, it doesn't!" Her voice raised a couple of eerie notches as Marissa got up into her face. "Why can't you see what I can? We were meant to be friends. I love your books and can offer my suggestions to make them even better in the future. Don't mess this up for us, Daphne." Her thin brows lowered over her narrowed eyes. "I won't let that cop come between us."

"What?" Daphne played innocent to her direct threat against Kenneth.

"You heard me," she snapped. "I've seen him with you. And I'm guessing he wants you to move here."

Her lower lip hung down angrily. "Where does that leave me as your number one fan? We both belong in Alabama. Not Hawaii."

I'm not sure where I belong anymore, Daphne told herself truthfully. If it was to be with Kenneth, she would know soon enough. What was clear, however, was that her stalker was unwilling to take no for an answer. Making her all the more dangerous. "I need time to think," she told her, hoping this would get her to leave long enough to have her arrested. "Can you give me that much?"

Marissa ran a sunburned hand through her hair thoughtfully. "Yeah, I can." Another pause, then a stark warning, "But don't take too long."

"I won't." Daphne pretended to play nice. "So, where are you staying?" That would make it easier to pass on to the police.

"Never mind," she snorted smartly. "I'm going… for now." She regarded her with a menacing stare. "See you later."

On that note, Marissa rushed out of the villa as if she had somewhere better to be. Daphne quickly locked the door and took a moment to get herself together. She had managed to avoid a confrontation that could have ended in disaster. But how long before Marissa came back, crazier than the last time? Or could she be taken into custody first?

Daphne went back into her interim office and grabbed her cell phone off the computer table. She punched the redial for Kenneth and when he answered, she said unsteadily, "You won't believe who just paid me a visit."

"Who?"

"Marissa Sheffield, my stalker from Alabama," Daphne made clear.

"Marissa Sheffield was there?" Kenneth asked in disbelief.

"Yes." Daphne raised her voice. "She tracked me to Maui," Daphne hated to say it. "What's more, she threatened us both." She sucked in a deep breath before stating flatly, "And I'm afraid she means business."

Chapter Thirteen

Kenneth's mouth was agape as he stood inside Daphne's villa before reiterating what he'd asked earlier on the phone, "Marissa Sheffield actually showed up here?"

"In the flesh," Daphne informed him. "She was standing right where you're standing now. Only it was much more unnerving."

"Sorry you had to go through that." More than he could say as Kenneth hated that the unstable stalker had given Daphne a whole new cause for concern on Maui.

"I thought you said Marissa never left Alabama?" Daphne's arms were folded petulantly.

"She hadn't," Kenneth defended his previous words. "At least not at that point. Somehow, she was able to evade tracking and make her way here."

"She's been following me...us," Daphne uttered. "Who knows for how long? Point is, she's clearly dangerous, Kenneth. Unless you arrest her for stalking and, I don't know, violating the conditions of her bail, there's no telling what she may be capable of."

"I agree," he spoke in earnest, troubled that the stalker had threatened him as well. "Which is all the more reason why I'd like you to stay at my place, with a security system, till we can find her. We've issued a BOLO for Marissa Sheffield, using both her mug shot and your description of her current look, and should be able to take her into custody in short order. Still, it's best to be on the safe side." Beyond that, Kenneth liked the idea of having Daphne close by as long as an elusive serial killer was also on the loose and even more of a threat to her health and well-being. If being accosted by a mentally unstable stalker could do the trick, so be it.

"Okay," Daphne relented. "Maybe it is a smart idea to not ask for trouble if I can possibly avoid it."

Kenneth wondered if there was a dual message in there somewhere. "I do have a spare bedroom that you're welcome to use, if you like." Far be it for him to presume she'd want to share his bed every night, and even during daylight hours, simply because it was something that worked for him for as long as she remained on the island. "I have no problem setting up boundaries, if that's what it takes to keep you out of harm's way."

"Boundaries aren't necessary," Daphne stressed. "But it's only fair that I have my own space, when needed. At least till we know where this is going between us."

"I understand," Kenneth told her. How could he not? After all, he was just as uncertain about what would become of them once she had completed her research and needed to return to the life she'd made for herself in Tuscaloosa. Would she welcome him there with open arms? Would relocating to Maui be out of the question for her when it came right down to it? Now was not the time to tackle those questions but rather get her to safer ground.

"Mahalo," Daphne uttered, stepping up to him and wrapping her arms around his waist. "We'll have a nice long talk once we're past all this unwanted drama."

"Yeah." He held her close, wishing it could last a lifetime. Maybe it could. If that drama, which included a demented stalker and diabolical killer, didn't swallow them whole. And with it, any hopes for the future.

"Any news on Marissa Sheffield?" Daphne asked Detective Vanessa Ringwald the following morning when she showed up at Kenneth's house.

Vanessa shook her head. "Not yet. We're checking all the local accommodations to see if she's staying at any of them. So far, nothing. But don't worry. She can't hide forever. We'll get her."

"Hope so." Daphne gave her a little smile, thankful that the detective had been nonjudgmental in finding her staying with Kenneth temporarily. Though the idea of it becoming a more permanent situation appealed to her on a serious level, Daphne didn't dare cross over into the realm of thinking prematurely.

For one, Kenneth hadn't invited her to stay. For another, the nature of what they meant to one another still had not been defined in terms beyond the surface. So she would wait, focusing instead on the moment at hand. Her stalker was out there somewhere, looking for another opportunity to come after her.

Kenneth, who was holding a mug of coffee as they stood in the kitchen, said, "Vanessa's right, Daphne. Now that we're onto Sheffield, it's only a matter of time before we track her down. In the meantime, I'm assigning an officer to remain outside in case she shows up here, my excellent security system notwithstanding. And should you want to go out, which I suspect is a given, to continue your work or whatever, he'll follow and keep an eye on you."

Daphne frowned. "Is that really necessary?" It almost felt like she was a prisoner rather than someone who made a good living writing about criminals who ended up in prison.

"I'm afraid so," Kenneth insisted. "Best not to take any chances that Sheffield could give us the slip and go for broke to get to you."

"He's right," Vanessa pitched in. "I've seen or heard about cases like this when obsessed stalker fans crossed over into homicidal maniacs."

Unfortunately, Daphne was also familiar with such incidences of stalking that ended in tragedy. The murder of musician John Lennon by Mark David Chapman and actress Rebecca Schaeffer by Robert John Bardo came to mind. She had no wish to become a fatality and yesterday's news by being defiant toward those who wanted to help keep her safe. "Fine," she told them. "Whatever you think is necessary."

Kenneth grinned at her. "Good."

Daphne got a warm feeling inside as she thought of them cuddling last night without the sex, illustrating that what they had went beyond carnal impulses. She smiled back at him and left it at that, while lifting up her mug of coffee from the slate countertop.

When her cell phone rang, Vanessa answered it with, "Ringwald," listened and told the caller, "We're on our way." Disconnecting, she turned toward Kenneth, a bleak look crossing her face. "There's been a report of a woman's body being found at the Lei Motel on Wharf Street in Lahaina. Appears as though she was suffocated with a plastic bag over her head."

For whatever reason, Daphne got a bad feeling that the victim was none other than her stalker, Marissa Sheffield. If true, the thought that she had fallen prey to a serial killer bothered Daphne, making her feel guilty for unwittingly bringing the obsessed fan to the island, resulting in the loss of Marissa's life.

IT WASN'T DAPHNE's stalker after all, Kenneth knew, as he studied the victim. She was slender and around five-six, sitting in a tufted armchair in the small motel room. Her narrow face was covered by a plastic bag, twisted in agony from being suffocated.

Long thin dark hair in a curly down style was swept to one side. She was fully clothed in a floral print V-neck ruched dress and block heel black sandals while wearing an orchid flower lei.

"According to her driver's license," Agent Noelle Kaniho said, "the victim's name is Ashley Gibson. The twenty-five-year-old lived in Westport, Connecticut. Her body was discovered by a housekeeper."

"Based on Ms. Gibson's clothes," Kenneth said, "I'd say she's been like that all night."

"Must have been a hell of a night," Agent Kirk Guilfoyle suggested sardonically. "Gibson had apparently been vacationing on the island, according to a front-desk worker, and was particularly keen on its nightlife."

Kenneth wondered if the killer had followed her from one of the hot spots. Or even left with her, unsuspecting of what was in store. He homed in on what looked to be a burn mark at the base of her throat. "He used the stun gun on her to gain complete control."

"Seems that way," Vanessa said sadly.

"There's no quitting with this guy," Guilfoyle bemoaned. "Not that I would expect the unsub to throw in the towel, as long as he can find victims to asphyxiate the life out of."

Kenneth furrowed his brow. "The Maui Suffocation Killer moniker has definitely gone to the perp's head," he speculated. "He's getting more and more brazen with each kill, putting us on notice that he's very much still in business and having fun in a maniacal fashion." Kenneth was thoughtful. "But since it's likely that we're looking for a man named Tommy, who we now have on video, along with a digital sketch, I think we're closing in on him, whether he likes it or not."

"You could be right about that," Noelle agreed. Putting on a nitrile glove, she lifted the victim's pale hand, studying the long, pink-colored fingernails. "Looks like there's dry blood beneath them. My guess is that it belongs to her attacker. Can you say DNA?"

"Yeah, definitely some DNA there," Kenneth agreed, "most likely from the unsub." Of course, he understood that even if that were the case, they still needed a match to identify the person.

They were joined by the medical examiner and coroner, who griped, "This is starting to get annoying."

"I think it's way past the starting point," Kenneth said, being real about it.

"You're right, unfortunately," Rudy Samudio admitted, putting on his latex gloves. He immediately began his preliminary examination of the decedent, noting the DNA beneath her nails. Afterward, he said, "I hate to sound like a broken record, but the victim almost certainly was killed due to asphyxia sometime between one and five a.m. But she did manage to scratch her assailant."

"Or in other words, Doc, we're talking about another victim of the serial killer?" Guilfoyle put forth.

Samudio nodded. "No reason to believe otherwise

at this point, given the similarities between the victims and manner of death. It'll be up to you guys to make the final call."

"It's been made for us," Kenneth spoke bluntly. "Now we just need to stop him before the next victim crosses his path."

As the crime scene technicians took over and interviews commenced with other motel guests and staff, Kenneth thought of Daphne, knowing she had feared the victim was the person stalking her. The fact that this possibility bothered Daphne so, in spite of the danger Marissa Sheffield posed, told Kenneth everything he needed to know about what a special woman Daphne was. Not that he hadn't already realized that before now. It only added to the growing number of reasons why he was crazy about her in a perfectly sane way. He stepped away and phoned her. "Just wanted you to know that your stalker wasn't the latest victim."

"I'm happy to hear that," Daphne uttered, "weird as that may sound."

"Doesn't sound weird at all," Kenneth told her. "You're not the type who would wish a horrible death on anyone. Not even Marissa Sheffield."

"You're right about that. She's become a real problem, but no one should have her life taken away at the hands of a serial killer."

"Sheffield has managed to avoid that fate, for now," Kenneth warned. "Hopefully, we'll find her before the perp manages to target her. Or your stalker takes another crack at threatening you."

"I'm with you on both fronts," Daphne said. "But I think you know that."

"I do." He was beginning to know her all too well and wouldn't have it any other way. "I have to go," he told her and reminded her to be careful while feeling comforted in knowing the muscular and veteran officer he had assigned to Daphne would be there to safeguard her should trouble come her way.

"ALOHA," FRANCIS HIRAGA said to Daphne over the phone, surprised to hear from him.

"Aloha," she responded.

"I don't know if you're interested in this or not, but I'm about to head over to the cemetery to pay a visit to Jenny's gravesite on the one-year anniversary of her death. I thought you might like to come for some added perspective when writing about the tragedy."

Daphne had not expected such an invitation. Her first thought was to pass, but then she remembered why she was on Maui in the first place. She couldn't allow the uneasiness of a stalker and a serial killer on the loose to cloud her judgment as a true crime writer unafraid to take chances. Surely, Kenneth understood that? Moreover, she did have Officer Jose Menendez ready to step in between her and danger. What little she knew of the six foot four brawny and baldheaded fortysomething widower with a horseshoe mustache was that he was a no-nonsense kind of guy and took his job seriously. That was good enough for Daphne as she felt the same about her occupation. She told Francis, "Yes, I would like to see where Jenny is buried." She assumed her mother, daughter, daughter's boyfriend and even Norman Takahashi himself were in the cemetery as well.

"Mahalo," Francis said and gave her directions. "See you soon."

Daphne texted Kenneth about her plans, then hitched a ride with Officer Menendez to the Heavenly Palms Cemetery on Waiale Road in Wailuku, following a slight detour to a local florist, where she purchased a bouquet of fresh lilies. "I'll be right here if you need me," Menendez told her, standing outside his vehicle. Daphne nodded and headed across the grass to the nearby gravesite, where Francis was placing red roses against the white marble headstone.

He lifted and turned when he heard her. "I appreciate you coming."

"Thanks for inviting me," she told him, and set the bouquet beside his flowers.

Francis bowed his head. "Nice of you to do that."

Daphne's eyes twinkled. She glanced at the gravesites of Sarah Takahashi, Donna Duldulao and Lucas Piimauna while noting that Norman Takahashi's grave was nowhere to be found. Gazing back at Francis, Daphne said thoughtfully, "I know how difficult this must be for you." Even now, whenever visiting her parents' graves, she grieved in wondering why their lives had to end in such a tragic way.

"It was a boy," Francis reflected on his unborn child. "We were going to name him Makoa, which means fearless and courageous in Hawaiian."

"It's a good name," Daphne said sincerely.

"Yes, I think so." Francis paused, staring down at his Oxford shoes. He looked up at her. "So, how's the research coming for your book?"

"I'm just about done with it," she answered. "At least the part I needed to do on the island."

"Good." He grinned. "If you want to take a picture of Jenny's grave for the book so people can always remember her, feel free to do so."

Daphne nodded to that effect, but declined, feeling it was unseemly, even if a common element of many true crime books. Some things, she believed, should be left alone.

"I saw you on television," he commented. "I thought you did a nice job talking about your books and the serial killer we're currently dealing with on Maui."

At the reference to the serial killer case, Daphne looked instinctively at Officer Menendez, who was watching them and wouldn't take long to close the gap if needed. Turning back to Francis, Daphne tried to picture him as the Maui Suffocation Killer, but somehow that didn't seem to be a good fit. Or could she be unwisely thrown off by him being an ER doctor who was supposed to save lives, not take them?

"Everyone's a little spooked by such a killer being loose on the island," she told him candidly. "True crime writers who happen to be female are no different."

"Is that why the officer is over there—to protect you?"

Daphne didn't deny it. "You could say that." She saw no reason to mention that the protection was more about a stalker than a serial killer, though knowing Kenneth, this was his way of trying to keep her safe from both offenders.

"Figured as much," Francis said. "Well, you're safe with me."

She gave him a confident smile. "Good to know."

"I will say that I was blown away when the man whose life I tried to save on the day we met, Ben Hoffman, was believed at that time to be the Maui Suffocation Killer."

Daphne smoothed a brow. "The evidence seemed to point toward that conclusion till the killings started again."

"And Hoffman wound up being a copycat killer," Francis contended.

"So it seems," she said musingly, not ruling out that Hoffman did what he did without any inspiration beyond his own homicidal impulses.

"This may sound odd, and I'm not even sure why I'm mentioning it, but on the day Roxanne Sinclair died, I had a voice-mail message from her asking if we could meet because we had something in common." Francis furrowed his brow. "She said she'd been having an affair with Norman Takahashi. Before I could call her to get together, she was dead and they said it was the work of the real Maui Suffocation Killer."

Daphne processed what he'd just said, again glancing at the officer and back suspiciously. "Did you tell this to the police?"

"No, I didn't think it was relevant to their investigation," he argued. "It was probably a bad move on my part."

"You think?" Her voice was thick with sarcasm.

Francis reacted. "Since I still have the voice-mail message, I'll send it to Detective Kealoha, who I hear is working the case."

"That's a good idea," she pressed, knowing Kenneth would want it as potential evidence. Daphne wondered if the doctor could have killed Roxanne as a way to get revenge for Takahashi killing Jenny. Or as the Maui Suffocation Killer getting back on track after Ben Hoffman's possible copycat killing took away from the serial killer's infamy.

Seeming to sense her misgivings, Francis took a step back and said, "Just in case you're wondering if I murdered Roxanne Sinclair, I can assure you I did not. I was stuck in the ER that entire day and well into the night. Pretty easy to verify. Same is true for last night, when I understand another young woman was killed."

"Okay." Daphne took him at his word, knowing that Kenneth would follow up on his alibi for both murders. She breathed a sigh of relief nevertheless as it appeared that Francis Hiraga was still grieving the loss of his lover, but was not a killer. Which indicated that someone else was out there continuing to mark women for death.

Chapter Fourteen

Probably the last person Kenneth, or Vanessa for that matter, expected to hear from was Zack Lawrence, the fitness instructor who had once been their number one suspect as the Maui Suffocation Killer. But given that he claimed to have information on the investigation, they had little choice other than to hear him out. Kenneth drove into the parking lot of the Wailuku Gym on Kolu Street owned by Lawrence as Vanessa muttered, "Think Mr. Casanova is just looking for some attention to stroke his ego?"

"We're about to find out," Kenneth said, trying to keep an open mind. "My guess is that Lawrence has no desire to stay on our radar by getting us over here just to mess with us."

"Hope you're right. We've got better things to do with our time than play games."

"You've got that right." Kenneth was certainly in no mood for games. Not when too many lives were at stake as long as a killer remained on the prowl and dangerous as ever.

They left the car and headed toward the gym, bordered by Golden cane palm trees. Inside, the large gym had all the latest equipment and was in full swing with users exercising. Kenneth spotted Zack Lawrence at an elliptical machine, flirting with a fit and tanned brunette-haired young woman, before he left her and approached them, wearing designer workout clothes and black cross-training shoes.

"Hey, thanks for dropping by," Lawrence said casually as if they were old friends.

"Gee, you're welcome," Kenneth responded wryly.

Lawrence grinned crookedly at Vanessa and said, "Nice to see you again, Detective Ringwald."

"Wish I could say the same," she stated, sneering at him.

"Why don't you tell us why we're here, Lawrence," Kenneth spoke impatiently, "and we'll be on our way."

"Yeah, sure." Lawrence looked around the gym. "Let's go to my office."

Kenneth eyed Vanessa and back. "Lead the way."

They went inside a spacious office with modern furnishings and a ceiling fan spinning. "Do you want to sit down?" Lawrence proffered his long arm at a rust-colored velvet sofa.

Both declined and Vanessa said hotly, "You said you have some information pertaining to our serial killer investigation."

"Yeah, I think so." He walked over to his ergonomic T-shaped standing desk and grabbed a sheet of paper, bringing it back over to them. "I happened to see this sketch of the suspect you're looking for on my laptop and realized that I know this guy."

"Really?" Kenneth glanced at the sketch and back.

"Well, not really. I mean, we weren't friends or anything," Lawrence said, shifting from one foot to the other. "I saw him at a couple of clubs where I hang out. At least it looks like the guy."

Vanessa pursed her lips. "You need to do better than that, Lawrence," she snapped. "Do you have anything worthwhile for us or not, beyond some less than convincing belief that he looks familiar?"

"All right, all right." Lawrence lifted his hands as if in mock surrender. "If it's the person I think he is, he came up to me one time and asked what my secret was for getting women. I told him there is no secret. It's as plain as day and tried and true over the centuries. Look good, smell good and give them what they want. Simple, really."

"I don't think so," she snorted. "Not all women fall for that, sorry."

"Don't be." He shrugged. "Win some, lose some."

While he was apparently charming more women than not, with Vanessa being the exception to the rule, Kenneth was much more interested in the other man. "How did he respond to this?"

"It angered him," Lawrence indicated. "He accused me of making it difficult for men like him. I said it was just the opposite. All you needed was to follow the formula and have confidence in yourself.

He didn't respond well to that, either." He rolled his eyes dismissively. "Some dudes just don't get it."

"Did he ever tell you his name?" Kenneth asked interestedly.

"Yeah, I believe he said it was Tommy."

Kenneth looked at Vanessa. The presumed name of the suspect had not been made public as yet. This appeared to give more fuel to the likelihood that this was the same man who had come to Daphne's book signing while fitting the description she and Ruth Paquin gave of the unsub.

"Did he give you his last name?" Vanessa asked.

"Just Tommy."

Kenneth peered at him. "Have you seen this Tommy at your gym?"

"No." Lawrence shook his head. "Not exactly the type who was into staying in shape, if you know what I mean. Still, I'm a believer that anyone can better themselves if they're willing to take that first step. So, I gave him my card."

"How generous of you," Vanessa said sarcastically.

Kenneth eyed him. "If you happen to run into Tommy again at a club or he decides to show up here, let us know."

"Count on it." Lawrence ran a hand along his jawline. "Is this guy really the serial killer every woman I know is freaking out over?"

"That's yet to be determined," Kenneth said truthfully. "We count on people like you to help us find him and possibly prevent someone else from dying."

Lawrence nodded. "I'll keep my eyes open," he promised. "And ask around, in case someone else I know has information to pass along about him."

To Kenneth, this would have to do. They left the gym with him feeling as though they had turned a corner in the pursuit of the suspect who went by the name Tommy and seemed to pose a clear and present danger to attractive women with long dark hair on the island.

Outside, Kenneth remarked to Vanessa, "You were a bit hard on Lawrence, don't you think?"

"Yeah, probably," she admitted. "It's not like he didn't have it coming. I've met too many men like him, including my ex, who thought they were all that and seemed to have no problem playing head games with women."

Kenneth understood that she still had a chip on her shoulder from being forced to raise a child alone after her ex-boyfriend absconded his obligations, but all men weren't like him, or Zack Lawrence for that matter. Kenneth suspected she knew that, even if feeling the need to vent. "At least Lawrence gave us more to work with in getting some perspective on this Tommy. If he's who we think he is, the man seems to be taking his own inadequacies out on his victims."

Vanessa frowned. "That's a scary thought."

"Which is why we need to locate him," Kenneth said, a sense of desperation in his voice.

"We'll find him," she said with determination.

As they headed across the parking lot, Kenneth got a call from Daphne. He answered casually, "Hey, how did it go at the cemetery?"

"It was interesting," she told him, piquing his curiosity.

"How so?" He glanced at Vanessa, who was checking her own phone.

"Francis Hiraga said he received a voice mail from Roxanne Sinclair on the day she died, hoping they could meet, given their common ground with Norman and Jenny Takahashi. Francis says they never met and apparently has an alibi for Roxanne's time of death," Daphne pointed out. "Anyway, he's supposed to contact you about this. I thought it might be relevant to the current investigation, one way or the other."

"It is," Kenneth assured her. "Thanks for the heads-up. We'll certainly look into this."

"Okay." Daphne paused. "So, how's the search for Marissa progressing?"

He noted the concern in her tone. "She was apparently spotted loitering outside a supermarket in Kahului. Seems as if we just missed her."

Daphne groaned. "She's hard to catch."

Sounds like someone else we're searching for, Kenneth told himself sourly. "That won't last," he promised, then thought to ask, "How's Officer Menendez's presence working out?"

"Good," she assured him. "He's doing his job, watching over me."

"Happy to hear that." Short of being with her around the clock himself, Kenneth believed that Menendez was a good man to have on the job till they were able to make some arrests.

"My editor's calling," Daphne said. "I should probably get this."

"You should." Kenneth wanted her life to go on as normally as possible under the circumstances thrust upon her. It would be better all the way around when they could operate without the cloud of homicides and stalking hanging over them. Then see where things went. "Bye," he said, and hung up.

"Everything okay with Daphne?" Vanessa asked.

Kenneth brought her up to date regarding the unexpected connection between Francis Hiraga and Roxanne Sinclair.

"Hmm..." Vanessa batted her lashes. "Talk about six degrees of separation."

"Yeah, I know. It's strange. Yet not so much," Kenneth said when thinking about it.

"Could Dr. Hiraga actually be involved some way in Sinclair's murder?"

"He claims to have an alibi for her time of death. We'll have a chat with him and see if there's cause for further investigation," Kenneth told her. "But as it stands, Hiraga doesn't fit the description of the unsub we're looking at, even if the Tommy name is a moniker."

"Good point," Vanessa said as they reached the car. "Still, the way this case is going, one never knows..."

"True enough." Kenneth acknowledged that it was troubling to see some symmetry between a closed case and one still very much open. Was there anything to it? Or was this merely playing into the hands of a ruthless serial killer seeking to add to his number of homicides?

In the car, Vanessa turned to Kenneth and said unevenly, "This is probably none of my business, but what's going on between you and the true crime writer?"

You're right, it is none of your business, he thought. Yet, Kenneth felt the question wasn't unreasonable, considering the time he had been spending with Daphne. He also had a good working relationship with Vanessa, ever astute, and also considered her a friend. "Daphne and I have hit it off," he replied candidly.

Vanessa chuckled teasingly. "Tell me something I don't already know."

Kenneth glanced at her and back to the road. "Guess it wasn't that hard to figure out. She's a wonderful person, beyond the bestselling author."

"Just as are you, Kealoha, beyond the hard-nosed police detective," she told him. "I think you make a great couple."

He grinned musingly. "Mahalo."

"I just hope you don't blow it," she warned.

"You and me both," he concurred behind the wheel. "Long-distance relationships can be tricky, though. Not that we've delved into that much as yet."

"Trust me, all relationships can be tricky," Vanessa said matter-of-factly. "That doesn't mean we don't do what's necessary to keep them going, if the connection's strong enough. I'm just saying."

Kenneth laughed. "I'll keep that in mind. Maybe you missed your calling, Ringwald. Psychologist might have been more apropos."

She chuckled. "Actually, I was thinking that crime writer might suit me. I certainly have my fair share of murder investigations to draw upon. But not till I log in a few more years of detective work to add to that. Anyway, we're talking about you, not me. Go with your heart and the rest will take care of itself. And that's my two cents."

"But worth its weight in gold," Kenneth told her sincerely, giving him more to ponder, with Daphne never leaving his thoughts for long and with good reason.

DAPHNE SPENT THE early afternoon on her laptop, doing an online question-and-answer session as a guest blogger for a popular true crime blog. She tried to keep her answers short and sweet but deep enough to hold the attention of viewers. It was a welcome detour from dodging stalkers and serial killers, though she felt confident that with the Maui PD searching for them, neither would be able to stay on the loose for very long. She knew that Kenneth, in particular, was doing everything in his power to take both into custody. Of course, with the unsub yet to be officially

identified beyond a man named Tommy, the hope
was that this could be accompanied by scientific
and other hard evidence to lead to an arrest and conviction of the serial killer of at least eleven women.

In spite of wanting to see Marissa Sheffield off the
streets and out of her life for good, Daphne did find
solace in the fact that she hadn't been the most recent victim of the Maui Suffocation Killer as Daphne
had feared. *I wouldn't wish that type of death on my
worst enemy,* she told herself. Troubled stalker or not.
But that hardly meant she wanted to give Marissa a
pass for following her to Maui and threatening both
her and Kenneth. Even though she was sure he could
take care of himself, Daphne didn't doubt that crazy
people were capable of doing crazy things, no matter the obstacles. As such, she wouldn't feel at ease
until her obsessed stalker had been located and the
threat was over.

Until such time, Daphne preferred to focus on
self-promotion and wrapping up the research needed
for her next book, *A Maui Mass Murder.* Beyond
that, there was still a strong possibility that once the
Maui Suffocation Killer investigation had come to a
conclusion, she would write about it as well, including the unexpected crossover of elements between
the two murder stories. She wondered how this might
fit in with things between her and Kenneth. Would
they be able to move forward at the end of the day?
Or would love not be enough to conquer any road-

blocks they would surely face if they were to make this work?

Feeling restless, Daphne put her hair up and threw on some jogging clothes, having checked out of the Kiki Shores Villas to stay at Kenneth's house, gladly accepting his invitation to do so as both a matter of practicality and an opportunity to be closer to one another. She peeked through the venetian blinds and saw that Officer Menendez was in his car on duty. Meaning that he would spot Marissa if she somehow showed up at the house.

Stepping outside, Daphne took in Kenneth's be-atific property before going for a jog, while marveling at the amazing views of Molokai and Lanai, along with the ocean itself. *If there truly is such a thing as paradise*, she thought, *this is pretty close to it*. She only wondered if that would be enough to keep her on Maui much longer.

Chapter Fifteen

After interviewing Francis Hiraga and checking out his alibi, Kenneth believed the doctor had nothing to do with the death of Roxanne Sinclair. Or, for that matter, the other serial killings, with Hiraga also able to account for his whereabouts. Still, Kenneth found it somewhat eerie that Hiraga and Sinclair were forever bound by Norman and Jenny Takahashi's infidelity and murder-suicide; with Sinclair now a victim of a serial killer, indirectly linking the homicide cases.

Oddly, Kenneth considered that, apart from writing a book on the Takahashi tragedy, Daphne had unwittingly become a part of his current investigation with the prime suspect, a man named Tommy, attending her book signing and potentially eyeing her as a victim. The fact that the unsub had killed Roxanne Sinclair shortly after she met with Daphne was equally troubling to Kenneth, giving him all the more reason to want to keep her safe, over and beyond protecting her from Marissa Sheffield.

I can't let anything happen to Daphne on my watch, he thought with determination, as Kenneth headed to the Police Department's Crime Lab on Wili Pa Loop in Wailuku. Not the way he felt about her. She needed to know just how strong those feelings had become before she left Maui. Then they could go from there as to how she responded, with his hope that it would be positive in moving ahead.

In the crime lab, Kenneth joined Tad Newsome in meeting with forensic analyst Farrah Ueto at her workstation. In her early thirties and of medium build, with jet black short hair in a blunt cut and small black eyes, she had recently worked in the Scientific Investigation Section of the Honolulu Police Department before transferring to the Maui PD. Wearing a white lab coat, she smiled at the detectives and said, "Aloha."

Kenneth, feeling antsy, cut right to the chase. "Were you able to come up with anything from the blood beneath Ashley Gibson's fingernails?"

"Yes," Farrah answered concisely. "We've collected the DNA that Ms. Gibson was able to get by apparently scratching the skin of her assailant deep enough to draw blood. It was not a match for the victim's own DNA, to be clear," she stated.

Newsome angled his face in anticipation. "So, who does it belong to?"

"Unfortunately, we don't have a name yet," Farrah told him. "The DNA profile was submitted to CODIS, hoping something would click in either the

Arrestee or Convicted Offender Indices or Forensic Index." She sighed. "So far, the Federal DNA Database Unit's search for a match has not made a hit."

Kenneth frowned, hoping that this Tommy's full name would surface, giving them a direct line to the suspect. "Guess we couldn't get that lucky," he spoke sardonically.

"Don't give up," Farrah told him. "As you know, these things can take a while. If the unsub is in the system, we'll find him, and then you can make an arrest."

"Can't happen soon enough," Newsome griped. "This killer doesn't know the meaning of taking a break. He needs to be stopped."

"We're doing the best we can," she said. "Just as you are. The moment I hear anything, I'll let you know."

"Okay," Kenneth said, realizing that she wasn't a magician at producing results that weren't there. But he sensed that the unsub's DNA would eventually lead to a breakthrough.

Farrah shared this thought when saying, "His DNA is bound to show up elsewhere. A serial killer can only hide his genetic code for so long. Given the number of people he's killed, it's amazing that his DNA hasn't already produced a match."

Newsome wrinkled his nose. "Yeah, I keep telling myself the same thing. Little good that's done."

Kenneth shared his frustrations while knowing they both understood how this worked. Even serial killers could delay the inevitable for a time. Only in this instance, there was precious little of it to waste before the unsub went after someone else.

"WE'VE GOT A situation here," Jared McDougall said mysteriously over the phone.

Kenneth, who was at his desk, sat up. "What is it?"

"A hiker passing through the north end of my property has discovered what appears to be human remains, half buried."

Kenneth reacted. "Can you tell if it's a male or female?"

"A shoe sticking out of the dirt suggests a female." Jared sighed heavily. "Needless to say, I'm pretty shaken up about it."

"I understand," Kenneth told him, pondering the sobering news. He hated that his friend should have to deal with something like this in retirement. Never mind the fact that someone was dead, likely the victim of a homicide. "We're on our way."

An hour later, a team of investigators had descended upon McDougall's ranch, homing in on the area in question that consisted mostly of weeds and dirt softened from recent rainfall. While waiting for the remains, still yet to be officially identified as human, to be unearthed, Kenneth took note of the gold ballet flat, darkened by dirt, that seemed to be about a size eight or eight and a half, and certainly appeared to be a woman's shoe.

When the remains were brought up, still intact, a

veteran forensic identification officer named Stefanie
Chadwick declared them to be those of a human
female. As he processed this, what first caught
Kenneth's attention was that the head of the badly
decomposed victim was covered by a clear plastic
bag. Wearing a red cold-shoulder top and high-rise
flare jeans, she was slender and, he estimated, about
five feet six inches tall with long dark hair. The other
ballet flat was still attached to her foot. The similarities between the female and the victims of the Maui
Suffocation Killer sent chills down Kenneth's spine.

With this section of the property now an official
crime scene, police investigators, FBI agents and
crime scene technicians combed the area for clues on
what, to Kenneth, was a homicide with far-reaching
implications. He estimated that the victim had been
deceased for months or more, possibly predating the
first known victim of the serial killer around eight
months ago. Were there more bodies buried? More
victims elsewhere on the island?

Kenneth walked over to the twentysomething female hiker, Gail Broderick, who made the grisly dis-
covery and was clearly shaken up by it. "I've run this
route, or close to it, with Mr. McDougall's permission, maybe three times a week," she said, her thick
red hair in a mini braided ponytail.

"Have you seen other hikers in the vicinity?"
Kenneth asked.

Gail shook her head. "Not that I can recall. I've
pretty much had the area all to myself, as I live just

up over the hill, and no one comes this way." She frowned. "At least I didn't think so. Who would do such a thing?"

Kenneth could think of one suspect, but saw no need to freak her out even more in saying that a serial killer may be responsible. And could even be one of her neighbors. "That's what I intend to find out," he promised her.

Minutes later, Kenneth caught up with Jared McDougall, who had just been interviewed by FBI Agents Noelle Kaniho and Kirk Guilfoyle. They were standing on grass near Jared's house.

"If you have any more questions," Jared told them toughly, "you know where to find me."

Guilfoyle nodded. "Fair enough."

As they walked away, Jared lowered the brim of his Western hat and said gruffly, "They're treating me like I'm the criminal."

"Just doing their job," Kenneth told him feelingly. He didn't believe for one moment that his friend had anything to do with the dead body found on his ranch as someone who had spent a good part of his life putting real criminals behind bars.

"Yeah, I know," he muttered acquiescently.

"Sorry about this, Jared."

"I can't believe someone used my land as a dumping or burial ground for this poor woman," he said, kicking his boot at the grass.

"Neither can I." Kenneth gazed across the land thoughtfully. "Depending on how long she's been dead, it could have preceded your ownership of the property."

"Yeah, there is that possibility. Still, the fact that it happened at all, and I'm left to deal with it, is a hard pill to swallow."

"I know." Kenneth's brow creased. "Even harder is that, considering the manner of death, she may have been murdered by the same unsub we think killed at least eleven other women."

"That thought crossed my mind, too," Jared said, running a calloused hand across his mouth. "If so, there has to be a way to stop him."

"We're working on it," Kenneth stated firmly, while knowing that only action at this point would suffice. Particularly if the culprit had just raised the stakes even more.

DAPHNE WAS SHOCKED to hear about the dead woman discovered on Jared McDougall's property. More disturbing was the apparent manner in which she died, being suffocated like the female victims of a serial killer. Was there a connection? Or were they two entirely different acts of criminality? "Do you know how long she's been dead?" she asked Kenneth as they stood on his back lanai.

"That will be up to the medical examiner to determine," he responded, holding a beer. "Judging by her condition, I'm guessing she's been dead for some time."

Daphne grabbed the beer bottle and took a drink

before handing it back to him. "Any idea who she is? I mean, has anyone been reported missing in the past few months or beyond that?"

Kenneth considered this. "We've had our fair share of women reported missing," he told her. "In most instances, it was simply a matter of miscommunication. Or the person showed up elsewhere, with a reasonable explanation. There was one local woman who went missing about a year ago. The search for her turned up empty."

"Could this be her?" Daphne wondered.

"Possibly," Kenneth said musingly, drinking beer. "She was in pretty bad shape, so it may take a while to make a positive identification."

"Do you think she could have been killed by the same unsub blamed for the suffocation deaths of those other women?"

"Too soon to tell," he said, a catch to his voice. "The similarities are certainly troubling, to say the least. If so, this would open a whole new can of worms. Hopefully, forensics can obtain DNA from the remains to give us some answers."

Daphne found her mind churning as a true crime writer, always willing to consider every angle. "If this was the work of the same serial killer, could the perpetrator be a ranch hand or other employee of Jared's?" After meeting the former detective, she saw him as an honorable man and couldn't imagine him being a killer. Much less a serial killer.

"We're looking into that," Kenneth admitted. "At

the moment, we're just trying to wrap our minds around this."

"I understand." She took the beer bottle from him again and sipped. "Did you speak with Francis Hiraga?" she asked curiously.

"Yeah. His alibi checked out." Kenneth took the bottle, drinking from it. "Also ruled out his involvement in the other serial homicides. Seems that Roxanne Sinclair contacting Hiraga that day was coincidental to her murder."

"Glad to hear that," Daphne spoke sincerely. She hated to think that the doctor could have been doubling as a homicidal maniac. Nor was she keen on having to mix and match her current book with a possible new one. "Anything new on Marissa?"

"Nope." Kenneth frowned. "Wherever she's holed up, Sheffield's keeping a low profile. But she won't be able to touch you. As soon as she resurfaces, we'll make an arrest."

"Okay." Daphne had to accept this, even if a part of her was still concerned that Marissa would make her move when least expected. What Daphne didn't know was just how far her crazy fan would be willing to take this. Or, for that matter, how Marissa would react if cornered by the police. *Hopefully, it can all end with no one getting hurt*, Daphne thought.

Kenneth turned her his way and took Daphne's mind off the dark side of human nature with a kiss. She welcomed this, feeling the need to be with him, returning the stirring kiss full-fledged. They took it to the bedroom, and made love with the same passions that had brought them together the other times. Daphne's emotions ran high and when things settled down, she was left to wonder how she could ever return to a life on the mainland that didn't include the entirely addictive, intelligent and sexy man she had fallen in love with.

AT THE MAUI PD's Forensic Facility in Wailuku on Wili Pa Loop, Kenneth watched as the medical examiner and coroner, Dr. Rudy Samudio, was performing the autopsy on the unidentified victim. "While sparing you the grisly verbal details of carnivores going to town on the decedent's remains and rigors of decomposition over a period of time, her actual death was caused by asphyxia that came from having the plastic bag over her head. Given that she was lying in a shallow grave, she was all but certainly a victim of homicide."

Kenneth winced at the sight of the corpse. "How old was she at the time of death?"

"I'd say between twenty-five and thirty years of age."

The age range fit as far as the victims targeted by the Maui Suffocation Killer. "Can you tell if she was sexually assaulted?"

"I need more time to assess that," he responded, "but as of now, I'm not seeing any indication that she was raped or sexually victimized."

"Were you able to collect any DNA?"

"Yes." He lifted the bones of her hand. "It appears as though there is blood beneath a couple of the nails, like she scratched her assailant. Samples of the DNA have been sent to the crime lab for analysis."

"Good." Kenneth could only hope the DNA had not been corrupted over time. "How long ago was she killed?" he asked acutely, his interest more than just in passing.

"Based on the condition of the remains, I estimate that she has likely been dead for anywhere from ten months to a year," Samudio said, examining the corpse while wearing latex gloves.

"Hmm…" Kenneth muttered. *That would make it two to four months before the first known victim of the serial killer*, he thought. Could there be another killer at large?

Samudio seemed to read his mind as the coroner said, "You're probably wondering if your Maui Suffocation Killer got started sooner than suspected. Well, that will take further investigation on both our parts, Detective. But if I'm basing it on the manner of death and the consistency with the murders attributed to a serial killer, I'd have to say it's a good possibility that we're talking about the same perpetrator. Now as to why he would bury this one and not the others, that will be up to you to figure out."

"We will." Kenneth nodded musingly. "When do you think you'll be able to make a positive ID of the victim?"

"We hope to be able to identify the decedent

through dental records," Samudio responded, "along with the victim's clothing and a ring she was wearing. These things take time, though. I'll keep you posted."

"Mahalo," Kenneth said, gazing again at the victim and wondering if she could speak to them in terms of clues left behind in identifying her killer. If so, Kenneth wanted to try and hear her loud and clear in helping to bring the unsub to justice. In the meantime, he had to entertain all possibilities as to who the victim was, who decided to take her life and if there was in fact a connection between this murder and the similar homicides currently being investigated.

I don't like where this is going, Kenneth told himself after departing the forensic facility and heading to his vehicle. Why the hell had a young woman ended up buried on Jared McDougall's ranch? Instincts told Kenneth that Jared's hands were clean. But could the same be said for those he employed? Could any of them have decided that the unidentified female's life was worthless? If so, did this feeling extend to nearly a dozen other women? Or had this been a one-off, much like the murder of Irene Ishibashi by Ben Hoffman, a copycat killer, while an actual serial killer remained at large and as dangerous as ever?

Kenneth drove off with these questions weighing heavily on his mind, while knowing that within them lay the answers that would tell him everything he needed to know in solving the case of the latest homicide victim as well as the pending homicides by suffocation that deserved resolutions.

Chapter Sixteen

In the conference room, Kenneth stood by the large touch-screen monitor for his latest update at the meeting of the Suffocation Serial Killer Task Force. He had packed a lot into this and as such wasted no time getting to the nitty-gritty of where things stood. "I don't think I need to convince any of you just how trying these past months have been in working this case. Though we're still not quite at the finish line just yet, the progress made leads me to believe that realization is imminent."

He used the stylus to put the face of an attractive dark-haired, blue-eyed woman on the screen. "Her name is Willow Hudson, age twenty-five," he said. "Last week, Ms. Hudson's remains were discovered on the property of our former colleague Jared McDougall's ranch in Makawao. She was positively identified through dental records, along with the clothing and a gemstone ring she wore when she went missing ten months ago." Kenneth put the image of this evidence on the screen for a moment or two before switching back to her picture. "At the time of her death, Ms. Hudson was employed by the Transportation Security Administration as a screen officer at the Kahului Airport. I'll get back to that later."

He took a breath before clearing the screen and saying, "The good news here is that, after a thorough search of Jared McDougall's property, no other human remains were found, leading us to believe that Hudson's death was a one and done insofar as the location to bury her remains." Kenneth furrowed his brow. "The bad news is we think that Willow Hudson was the first victim of a serial killer named Tommy, and given the moniker the Maui Suffocation Killer by the media, whom we believe murdered twelve women in total by suffocating them with a plastic bag."

He put all the victims' images on the screen together, allowing that tragic reality to settle in before removing all but the faces of two victims. "Through CODIS and the Federal DNA Database Unit, DNA taken from beneath the fingernails of Ashley Gibson and Willow Hudson, the presumed most recent and first victim of the serial killer, were a match. Meaning that the DNA belonged to the same person, whom we believe to be the killer of both women."

Kenneth frowned. "Unfortunately, as good as this news is, it still does not identify the unsub by name. Apparently, up to this point, he's been able to avoid arrest or conviction, where his DNA would have provided an identification." Using the stylus, Kenneth brought up the image of a white male with dark hair in a mushroom cut, brown eyes and a medium build. "His name is Emerson Thomas Gladstone, age thirty-seven. Approximately two months before Willow Hudson went missing, Gladstone was employed at the Kahului Airport as a ramp agent. After Hudson accused him of sexual harassment, Gladstone was fired and said to be bitter because of it. Prior to his stint at the airport, Gladstone was employed as a ranch hand at the very property Jared McDougall owns, but before he purchased the ranch. We think Gladstone had it in for Willow Hudson and this killing mentality escalated in targeting other women of similar physical characteristics."

Kenneth sighed. "We believe that Emerson Thomas Gladstone was selectively using a version of his middle name, Tommy, such as when he attended a book signing by true crime writer Daphne Dockery." He showed the surveillance video of the suspect at the signing, then put up the digital sketch of the unsub with a split screen of Emerson's photo ID while an employee at the Kahului Airport. They were nearly identical. "Gladstone, or Tommy, was aptly described by Ruth Paquin, the only known victim of the killer to survive, as well as by Ms. Dockery and even Zack Lawrence, our original prime suspect as the serial killer.

"To shorten this long story, we believe we have more than enough probable cause to get a search warrant to collect Gladstone's DNA and look for other evidence," Kenneth pointed out. "And to make an arrest, pending the results of our findings."

Martin Morrissey, second in command of the Investigative Services Bureau, stood and said in a booming voice, "You've made your case, Kealoha, and a compelling one at that. You'll get the warrants. Bring Gladstone in before he can do any more harm on the island."

"You got it!" Kenneth took that as a good sign. Now they needed to finish this once and for all. Certain that Emerson Thomas Gladstone was the Maui Suffocation Killer who had terrorized women on Maui for months on end, it was past time to hold him accountable for his crimes of violence. Then Kenneth could turn his attention to the woman he hoped to spend the rest of his life with as his wife and mother of his children, sharing an all-around happy existence together wherever they lived. But first things first. They needed to apprehend a serial monster.

DAPHNE HADN'T PLANNED THIS, but she decided to actually begin writing her next true crime book, *A Maui Mass Murder*, while still on the island. With the research completed and an outline written, it seemed a good idea to do the first few chapters in the comfort of Kenneth's house. She had converted one of his spare bedrooms into a temporary office, which he had encouraged her to do. Though she was a little homesick, they both wanted to spend more time getting to know one another if they were to have any chance at turning what they had forged into a lasting relationship.

Tuscaloosa isn't going anywhere, Daphne told herself as she stopped typing on the laptop to gaze out the large window, where palm trees were swaying and the otherwise tropical setting was inspiring to her as a writer. But she knew that she couldn't remain in Hawaii forever. At least not as long as Kenneth appeared to drag his feet in exactly where he saw things heading for them. Or was she expecting more from her dream man than his reality?

I won't overthink this, she thought. What they had was real. Even if some things still needed to be ironed out like dress fabrics and shirts. She needed to be patient and let things move at their own pace. Fortunately for her, Daphne didn't need to wait to be in touch with her feelings for Kenneth. She was certain that the rest would soon take care of itself.

When she heard a sound outside the room, Daphne assumed it was either the house settling or the wind echoing within, as was often the case. She got up anyhow to check it out, padding across the hardwood floor in her bare feet. At a glance, she didn't see or hear anything else out of the ordinary. *Guess it was nothing*, she mused. Still, though she felt safe there with Officer Menendez outside, along with Kenneth's often masculine presence, something nagged at Daphne that just didn't quite set well with her. Call it women's intuition. Writer's awareness. Or whatever.

She peeked out the window and saw Menendez sitting in his car. No indication that anything was wrong. Yet, why did she feel otherwise? Perhaps it was because her stalker, Marissa Sheffield, had somehow remained at large for days since their encounter, as though biding her time before coming out of the woodwork and going on the attack. Even more troubling to Daphne was that the serial killer named Tommy, who Kenneth had identified as Emerson Thomas Gladstone, a former airport ramp agent, was apparently still on the loose as well. Though his arrest for the murder of Willow Hudson and eleven other women was impending, neither Daphne nor any women on the island could afford to take this for granted. Or lower one's guard.

As Daphne contemplated this and whether or not she should go check on Officer Menendez, or call Kenneth, the power suddenly went off. Fortunately, it was in the afternoon and sunny, so there was no difference in the lighting inside. She wondered if there had been a power outage in the area. Or was it just this house?

I better speak with Officer Menendez and see what's going on, Daphne thought nervously. She stepped into some slip-on flats while haphazardly putting her hair into a low and loose ponytail. The moment Daphne opened the door and gazed directly at the person on the other side, she realized it had been a very big mistake.

WITH ARREST AND search warrants in hand, members
of the task force and Special Response Tactical Team
arrived at Emerson Thomas Gladstone's apartment
complex, Beaubien Gardens, on Lower Honoapiilani Road in Lahaina. There was no sign of the suspect's red GMC Terrain Denali SUV. Believing that
he could still be inside, no one was about to take any
chances of running into an ambush. While wearing a
bulletproof vest, Kenneth took out his Glock 17 pistol
from its holster and led the way toward the ground
floor unit. He banged on the door and shouted that
they were there to execute a search warrant, hoping
it would be the ticket inside to apprehend the suspect.

When this was repeated and there was still no
response, Kenneth gave the order to use a battering
ram to force open the door. As they stormed inside
the one-bedroom apartment and across ceramic tile,
he noted the sparse contemporary furnishings and
untidiness of the place. On a lift-top wooden storage
coffee table, Kenneth spotted a copy of Daphne's true
crime book, *The Accident Killer*, bringing him back
to the unsettling thought of the serial killer suspect
being at her book signing. The idea that she had been
sized up by him for victimization grated on Kenneth.

"It's clear," Vanessa told him. "Whether Gladstone
had a sixth sense or just got lucky, he's not here."

Kenneth frowned, though having suspected as
much. "He won't get very far."

"Look what we've got here." Agent Noelle Kaniho

came into the room holding with nitrile gloves three firearms. "Found these ghost guns in the bedroom."

"Not surprised that the perp would have illegal weapons," Kenneth remarked of the unregistered firearms that had no serial numbers.

"There's more where those came from," Agent Kirk Guilfoyle said. "In a storage closet, Gladstone has stashed three short-barreled ghost gun rifles, a couple of high-capacity magazines and several double-bladed knives, among other things. Looks as though the man is getting ready for war."

"All the more troubling." Kenneth sighed, realizing the suspect was a greater threat than any of them realized. Not to say that being a certified serial killer wasn't bad enough. It was to Kenneth, and stopping Gladstone cold was front and center for him. "We need to put out a BOLO for Gladstone and his vehicle."

"It's done," Tad Newsome stated. "By the way, we found crystal meth and marijuana in the bathroom. Gladstone's some piece of work."

"Yeah, right." Kenneth rolled his eyes with disdain. "An extremely treacherous piece of work."

"And one whose DNA we now have," forensic analyst Farrah Ueto declared. She was holding two evidence bags with latex gloves. "Took the suspect's toothbrush and used razor. Between the two items, we should be able to extract DNA that can be compared with the matching DNA profiles from an unidentified perpetrator taken from underneath Ashley

Gibson and Willow Hudson's fingernails to see if there's a hit."

"Good work," Kenneth told her. "Go get it done and get the results."

"Will do," she promised.

"In the meantime," Kenneth said, his tone deepening to illustrate the level of heightened concern, "all things considered, we have to assume that Emerson Thomas Gladstone is in fact the Maui Suffocation Killer, and is armed and extremely dangerous. Every second he remains on the loose puts someone's life in danger."

In Kenneth's mind, that included Daphne, which was all the extra incentive he needed to go after Gladstone as though his own life depended on it. That mentality was put to the test minutes later when, while on the road, he got a call from Vanessa, who said in an urgent voice, "Gladstone's SUV has been spotted on Highway 30, not far from your place. It may not mean anything, but just thought you should know while we attempt to bring him in."

"Thanks, Vanessa," Kenneth said into the speakerphone as he tried to keep his heart rate steady. "Officer Menendez is stationed outside the house. In any event, I'm just minutes away, so I'll stop and make sure everything's fine. When you catch up to Gladstone, let me know."

"I will," she assured him before disconnecting.

In spite of wanting to believe otherwise, Kenneth had a gut feeling that the suspect's presence

near his house may not have been coincidence. He
tried to call Menendez for some reassurance but only
got the officer's voice mail. "Come on, pick up!"
Kenneth pleaded out loud. When there was no answer, he knew something was wrong. Gladstone,
or Tommy, was going after Daphne and Menendez
stood in his way.

While calling for backup and emergency medical
services to come to his house, Kenneth pressed down
on the accelerator, knowing full well that it might
be left up to him to save Daphne's life. And in the
process, give him and his one true love a chance at
a lifetime of happiness.

BEFORE DAPHNE COULD react, she felt the stun gun
placed on her neck, sending electrical shocks and intense pain throughout her body. Her brain suddenly
turned to mush and her arms and legs went limp as
she collapsed into the robust arms of her grinning
attacker, Emerson Thomas Gladstone. "Nice to see
you again, Daphne Dockery," he said amusingly. "In
case you've forgotten from your book signing, my
name's Tommy."

He chuckled and Daphne felt herself being dragged
roughly across the floor and pulled up onto the sectional sofa, where she was put into a sitting position,
which she could neither prevent nor control. "Oh, and
in case you're wondering about Officer Menendez,
he's incapacitated at the moment." Gladstone laughed
sarcastically as he knelt down to eye level with her.

"Couldn't allow him to interfere with my plans for you, Daphne. You see, ever since I read your book, I knew that I wanted you to join the other good-looking women with long dark hair in death. It's a perfect fit to have a true crime author essentially write her own story for another author to tell one day."

Gladstone chuckled at his own morbid sense of humor and Daphne realized she was unable to speak and couldn't clearly comprehend what he was saying to her. She still retained enough in her head to know that he was a serial killer intent on killing her. If only she could make herself think clearly and move her limbs freely, which were trembling involuntarily. *I don't want to die*, Daphne managed to think. But with Menendez unable to come to her rescue and no ability to contact Kenneth for help, her chances of survival were getting lower with each passing second.

"Before you breathe your last breath very soon now, Daphne," Gladstone said, as he removed a clear plastic bag from the pocket of his gold twill jeans, "which, trust me, will be even more painful than what you're experiencing now, I may as well tell you that it all started with that bitch Willow Hudson. She cost me my job, when all I wanted to do was get to know her. I made her pay dearly for that. Never thought they would ever find her body, but I guess I didn't bury her deep enough to keep the critters at bay."

He laughed. "The other women, including your-

self and Roxanne Sinclair, who I couldn't resist killing after she met with you, and to throw you and the
cops off balance in trying to figure out just who was
responsible, reminded me of Willow, as good-looking snobs or otherwise thought they were hot stuff.
And how ordinary guys like me are always ignored
by and we're sick of it. I know I am. You're about to
join the others, and Detective Kealoha will find your
corpse waiting for his return. I'd love to see the look
on his face, but I'll be long gone by then. Say hello
to Willow and Roxanne for me, Daphne."

He pulled the plastic bag over her head and face
and Daphne immediately gasped for air, her lungs
on fire. She felt dizzy and even more disoriented,
her body aching, when someone came up behind
Gladstone and pepper-sprayed him in the face and
eyes. As he bolted to his feet, bellowing while rub-
bing his eyes, someone apparently used his own stun
gun on him, pressing it into his throat as Gladstone
went down.

His attacker quickly yanked the plastic bag off
Daphne's head and she fought to catch her breath and
regain her equilibrium as the normal feeling began
to return to her brain and body.

Gladstone's attacker went back and used the stun
gun again on the serial killer, as though to pay him
back in some small measure for his heinous crimes.
Only as she gained clarity and heard the person
say, "I wasn't about to allow that creep to hurt you,
Daphne. Unlike his other victims. Sorry I couldn't

get here sooner," did Daphne realize that the improbable person to come to her rescue was none other than her obsessed stalker fan, Marissa Sheffield.

"Marissa..." Daphne managed to get out of her mouth in utter disbelief.

"Yeah." She smiled. "It's me. I tried, but just couldn't stay away."

Even as she tried to process this and get her feet to move, Daphne realized before Marissa did that Emerson Thomas Gladstone had recovered enough from the pepper spray and stun gun and become a threat again. Only, this time, he likely would want to kill them both.

KENNETH ARRIVED AT his house and saw Officer Menendez slumped over the steering wheel. He opened the driver's side door and checked his pulse. He was still breathing, having apparently been shot in the neck, something his bulletproof vest was unable to prevent. "Hang in there, buddy," Kenneth told him sorrowfully. "Help is on the way."

Leaving him, Kenneth recalled seeing Gladstone's SUV parked just down the road. No doubt for a quick escape. *Please don't let me be too late to stop him from killing Daphne, the woman I love*, Kenneth told himself, sickened at the thought of losing her to that madman. When he got to the back of the house, he could see that the power line had been cut, knocking the security system out. By the time the security monitoring company would have sent someone over to have a look, the damage would already be done. Daphne would be dead.

Slipping quietly through the back door with his sidearm out, loaded and ready to use, Kenneth could hear Daphne utter, "You won't get away with this, Tommy," though her words were a little incoherent. This told him that Gladstone had likely used the stun gun on her.

As Kenneth anguished over this and what else the creep might have done to her, he heard another female's unfamiliar voice say, "Leave Daphne alone. Kill me instead."

Kenneth recognized from her mug shot that the woman was none other than Marissa Sheffield, Daphne's obsessed fan. What was she doing in his house? He didn't get the sense that she had come there with Gladstone. Or was necessarily a threat to Daphne at this moment.

Once he had Gladstone clearly in sight, Kenneth could see him brandishing what looked to be a .40-caliber semiautomatic gun. Daphne placed herself between Marissa and Gladstone and told him firmly, "Let her go, Tommy. It's me that you want."

There was mocking laughter from Gladstone, who said smugly, "Thanks for offering to be her sacrificial lamb, but I think I'll take two for the price of one."

Kenneth begged to differ. "I wouldn't count on that," he snapped, approaching him with his gun aimed at his head. "You're under arrest, Emerson Thomas Gladstone, for too many crimes to mention at the moment. Drop the gun and put your hands up. Now!"

"I don't think so," Gladstone retorted defiantly.

In a swift move, catching Kenneth off guard, he turned the gun on him and fired. In a split second, Kenneth dove to the floor, but kept his own pistol aimed at the suspect. Under normal circumstances, he would have taken the offender out with one clean shot between the eyes. But this wasn't a normal situation. The last thing he wanted was to have to kill someone under his own roof. Especially when he intended to ask Daphne to live there. And so, in that instant of reflection and quick decision-making, Kenneth fired two bullets in rapid succession. One hit Gladstone squarely in the shoulder of his shooting arm, the bullet tearing through it, causing the gun to fly out of his hand. The second shot hit him smack dab in the kneecap, shattering his right leg in the process.

As Gladstone howled like a wounded animal and went down in a heap of anguish, Kenneth scrambled to his feet and rushed toward him like a man possessed as Gladstone tried to stand. Tackling him and bringing him down hard, Kenneth spat again, "You're under arrest, Tommy," and clocked him with a solid blow to the jaw, knocking him out stone-cold.

Not trusting that to last for long, Kenneth handcuffed him and stood, only to find Daphne running into his arms. "Is he going to live?" she asked shakily.

"Yeah, he'll live," Kenneth assured her confidently. "Gladstone's not about to get off that easily by dying before spending decades behind bars."

"Good." Daphne winced. "Thought I'd lost you for a moment there," she uttered.

"Not a chance." Kenneth ignored some aches and pains he felt from dropping to the floor as well as taking Gladstone down and landing awkwardly on top of him. "I was thinking the same thing about you," he admitted while checking her out. He could see a small burn mark on her neck from the stun gun.

"I'm fine," she insisted, touching the spot self-consciously.

"We'll get you checked out, anyway," he told her, sensing she had been put through more than met the eye. Daphne didn't argue the point.

Both looked toward Marissa, who suddenly looked like a lost deer in the woods. "What about her?" Kenneth asked warily, wondering how she had managed to evade capture, only to choose now to reappear as someone who seemed intent on stalking Daphne. "Or do I want to know?"

As Daphne struggled to find words, the front door burst open and Vanessa and Newsome ran in with their guns drawn. Agents Guilfoyle and Kaniho followed, along with members of the Special Response Tactical Team.

"One suspect is down," Vanessa stated while glancing suspiciously at Marissa.

"But apparently not for the count," Guilfoyle said in assessing Gladstone's condition.

She smiled satisfyingly. "That's good to hear."

"The sooner he's out of my house, the better," Kenneth told them in a huff.

"EMS should be here any moment now," Vanessa stated.

Kenneth nodded, though frankly he was more interested in making sure Jose Menendez pulled through and that Daphne was given a clean bill of health after her ordeal.

Newsome went to Marissa and, without being privy to the full story, placed her under arrest as a wanted fugitive stalker. Seemingly accepting her fate, Marissa put up no struggle. She looked at Daphne and said contritely, "I'm sorry."

Daphne met her gaze and voiced quietly, "Thank you." After she was led away and they were given a moment alone, Daphne uttered, "I want to help Marissa."

Kenneth raised a brow. "Really?" *What am I missing?* he thought.

"She saved my life," Daphne told him. "Tommy or Emerson Thomas Gladstone tried to suffocate me to death, just like the other women he went after. He confessed to it all like this was just a disgustingly sick game to him, as some type of payback against women who bore some resemblance to Willow Hudson after she rejected his advances. I honestly thought I was going to die." Daphne sighed. "Whatever her faults as a fanatical admirer, if Marissa hadn't shown up out of nowhere when she did…"

"Then I might not have been given the chance to

tell you that I'm deeply in love with you, Daphne, and want you to stay on Maui as my wife," Kenneth said, deciding there was no better time than now to lay his heart on the line. He was also grateful that, against all odds, Marissa Sheffield had swooped in like an angel and saved the day. *Will wonders never cease?* he mused.

Daphne met his eyes affectionately. "You do?"

He held her gaze in earnest. "Yes. At least for the next few years till I can put in for an early retirement," he explained. "Then we can move to Alabama, Alaska, hell, even Australia, if you want. Just so we're together and can have a good environment to raise a family, with as many children as you want." He knew she would be a great mother, whether they had one, two, three kids or more.

She took an agonizingly long moment before Daphne flashed a brilliant smile and said vivaciously, "Yes, I'd be delighted to live on the island as your wife and be the mother of our children, Kenneth. Since I'm also very much in love with you, I wondered just how long it would take for you to ask me to stay."

"Is that so?" He threw his head back with an amused laugh. "Apologies for keeping you waiting." But hearing her say she loved him made it well worth the wait as far as he was concerned.

"Apology accepted." She wrapped her arms around his neck. "With respect to someday living in Alabama, Alaska, Australia or elsewhere, I think not.

Who wouldn't want to live in Hawaii, on Maui, for a lifetime of joy with my handsome husband, even after you retire from the Maui Police Department, which doesn't need to be anytime soon? Island living may not always be perfect, with the likes of such frightening criminals as Norman Takahashi and Emerson Gladstone marring the Maui landscape from time to time, but true paradise is what you make of it. Right? From where I'm standing, we can make the most of it for many, many years to come."

"Well said," Kenneth told her endearingly. "Yeah." He kissed her on the mouth passionately and then looked her in the eye. "I fully intend to hold you to that for the rest of your life, Daphne Dockery."

She beamed and declared lovingly, "I wouldn't have it any other way, Mr. Kealoha," while punctuating this with another solid kiss.

Epilogue

Three months after Emerson Thomas Gladstone's reign of terror on Maui had come to an end, the Suffocation Serial Killer Task Force had finally been able to close the case and disband. On a Friday night, Kenneth and Daphne went out for celebratory drinks with Vanessa Ringwald, Noelle Kaniho, Tad Newsome, Kirk Guilfoyle and Martin Morrissey at a popular hangout for law enforcement called Ngozi's Bar on Lower Main Street in Wailuku.

"Never doubted we'd nail the bastard," Morrissey argued over his mug of beer.

"Not even a little doubt?" Kenneth teased him, appreciating the pressure they had all been under. But it was never so overwhelming that any of them were prepared to ever throw in the towel and allow evil to prevail.

"None," the Assistant Chief of Investigative Services Bureau maintained. "Not with the experienced and tenacious team we put together."

"I agree wholeheartedly," Kenneth had to admit, tasting his beer.

"Same here," Guilfoyle voiced loudly. "Gladstone was never going to get away with it. Or keep the killings going."

"Not a chance," Newsome went on the record while drinking beer. "Perps like him are always too confident for their own good."

Kenneth nodded, "Till biting off more than they can chew as it relates to violent criminal behavior."

"He'll need a full stomach for where he's headed," Morrissey laughed.

Vanessa grinned. "Getting a helping hand from a terrific true crime writer who definitely knows her stuff didn't hurt matters any," she said, raising her beer mug to Daphne.

"Hear, hear!" Noelle sang, lifting her beer mug as well, with everyone else following suit.

Daphne blushed. "Not sure just how much of a hand I gave, but hanging out with this guy," she said, pointing to Kenneth beside her at the table, "made it hard not to want to be involved on some level with getting to the root of the crime story." She drank beer. "That's not to say being targeted by a serial killer was anything I would have ever volunteered for."

While this elicited chuckles from the group, Kenneth could only manage a sideways grin. Knowing just how close she came to becoming another victim of Emerson Thomas Gladstone made Kenneth practically nauseous. But the fact that she had survived gave him joy beyond words. "Believe me, Daphne, I never wanted you to have to come face-to-face with Gladstone and in my own house, no less," he said sincerely.

"You had no way of predicting his moves or malicious mind at work," she reasoned.

Kenneth allowed this much. "Beating him at his own game, though, is something we can both take pride in."

"I couldn't agree more," Daphne stated, smiling warmly, and then gave him a kiss to back it up.

"Music to my ears." Kenneth savored this and took a moment to reflect on the investigation. As it turned out, the DNA found on Gladstone's toothbrush and razor had proven to be a perfect match for DNA taken from the suspect. In turn, CODIS had successfully linked the previous unknown DNA left under the fingernails of murder victims Willow Hudson and Ashley Gibson, the first and last victims of the Maui Suffocation Killer, to Emerson Thomas Gladstone. Along with being fingered for attempted murder by surviving victims, Ruth Paquin, Jose Menendez, Marissa Sheffield and Daphne Dockery, and additional physical, documentary and digital evidence to that effect, Gladstone faced charges of illegal firearms and drug-related offenses. It was all more than enough to convince him to plead guilty. In the process, he spared his victims' families and friends from having to relive their nightmares in court.

Kenneth was happy to be able to put this trying investigation behind him to the extent possible, knowing that the effects of such a case that had shattered so many lives would not simply disappear just like that anytime soon. The one person who gave him solace through it all was Daphne, his fiancée and best friend. After never getting the chance to see if things might have worked out between him and Cynthia Suehisa, he couldn't be more excited to make a life with Daphne, who embodied all the qualities he could have asked for in a future wife and mother of his children. In turn, he intended to give her everything he had to be a great husband and father, making his own parents proud in the Hawaiian tradition.

When he'd accompanied Daphne to Tuscaloosa a month ago, Kenneth was more than a little impressed with her upscale townhouse and its rustic furnishings, located near the University of Alabama. Had she wanted to keep it, he would have understood perfectly, only wanting her to be happy rather than homesick. But with her parents having been cremated and no real reason to stay in Alabama, Daphne had insisted that putting the place up for sale and moving to Hawaii was the best thing for her, both personally and professionally. Besides, Daphne knew she could always come back to visit her Aunt Mae and other relatives and friends whenever she liked, with his encouragement.

"Being with you is all I could ask for at this point

in my life," Daphne told him persuasively once they left the bar and went back to his house alone.

"I feel the same," Kenneth said, knowing what they had hardly came along every day. He'd seen enough relationships go off the rails before ever getting a chance to blossom. He intended to make sure that never happened with them, no matter what it took.

"Then we'll make the most of each and every day," she said, holding his hands. "That's sure to keep things interesting."

"I'm all about interesting." He gave her a kiss while already thinking of ways to make that line of thought hold up. "And making the days and nights count."

Daphne chuckled. "I guess we understand each other."

"Agreed. Like reading between the lines of a good book by a certain author," he said jokingly.

"I'll go with that." Her blue-green eyes lit and Kenneth took the ball and ran with it, knowing she was a dream he never wanted to wake up from.

AT THE ALOHA Land Bookstore in Lahaina, wearing an orchid in her hair and plumeria lei around the neck, Daphne Dockery Kealoha sat on the uncomfortable wooden chair signing copies of her latest true crime bestseller, *A Maui Mass Murder*. The tragic tale of mass murder and suicide had received rave reviews and Daphne was grateful to have an editor, Gordon Yung, and publisher that she worked so well with. But she felt even more blessed to be married to a wonderful man for the past nine months, Detective Kenneth Kealoha. Relocating from Tuscaloosa, Alabama, to Lahaina, Hawaii, on the island of Maui, had been everything she hoped it would be, and more. For Daphne, having fun on land and in the water with her husband was a priority, along with the adventurous joys of romance, in spite of the demands of their busy professional lives. They had made plans to start a family after Daphne's next book tour this summer and she couldn't be more excited while trying to decide if she wanted their first child to be a boy or girl.

She gazed up at the handsome face of the last person waiting in line for an autographed book and asked in a level voice, "What would you like me to say?"

He thought about it before responding nonchalantly, "Oh, how about to Ken, the world's greatest husband and most adorable fan?"

Daphne blushed at her husband. "I think I can manage that." She thought about Marissa Sheffield, her onetime obsessed fan, who had stalked her last year before saving Daphne's life in a totally unbelievable and brazen confrontation with serial killer Emerson Thomas "Tommy" Gladstone. After her arrest, Marissa had immediately gone into therapy. Daphne footed the bill, with the criminal charges being dropped in light of her heroic efforts and successfully dealing with her mental health issues. Though Marissa was still a fan of her books, Daphne was happy to see it had toned down considerably to a normal level and from a safe distance.

As for Tommy Gladstone, Daphne was already more than halfway through her next true crime book about the infamous serial killer titled *The Maui Suffocation Killer*. Gladstone had survived his injuries from being shot twice, as had Officer Jose Menendez, who had made a miraculous recovery and was now back at work full-time. Gladstone, who was spending the rest of his life behind bars at the Halawa Correctional Facility on Oahu, had surprised Daphne by granting her an exclusive interview. In spite of still having flashbacks of her ordeal while in his clutches, she had jumped at the opportunity, wanting to get greater insight into the mind of a psychopath that would make for a better book for true crime readers and criminologists alike. Moreover, Daphne had chosen to donate a generous portion of her royalties to organizations that offered support to the families of victims of serial killers, believing it was another way to give back to society.

Daphne wrote in the book and handed it to Kenneth. He looked at it and said sweetly, "Mahalo." He grinned at her while sporting a new look with his short curly locks in a brush back, mid-fade haircut. "What do you say we get out of here, Mrs. Kealoha?"

"That's a great idea, Mr. Kealoha." Daphne beamed and got to her feet, flipping her long hair to one side. She gave Kenneth a kiss and asked, "So, where would you like to go?"

"Oh, let me see…" He put a hand to his chin thoughtfully. "How about your place? Or mine?"

She showed her teeth. "How about *our* place?" At least for a while, though they had already begun to make plans for having a new house built in Upcountry Maui.

"That works." Kenneth smiled back, sliding an arm around her thin waist lovingly. "Let's do it."

"Thought you'd never ask," Daphne teased him as they went home.

* * * * *

In case you missed the previous books in R. Barri Flowers's Hawaii CI miniseries:

The Big Island Killer
Captured on Kauai
Honolulu Cold Homicide

You'll find them wherever Harlequin Intrigue books are sold!

Get 4 FREE REWARDS!

We'll send you 2 FREE Books plus 2 FREE Mystery Gifts.

FREE Value Over **$20**

Both the **Harlequin Intrigue®** and **Harlequin® Romantic Suspense** series feature compelling novels filled with heart-racing action-packed romance that will keep you on the edge of your seat.

HARLEQUIN
PLUS

Try the best multimedia subscription service for romance readers like you!

Read, Watch and Play.

Experience the easiest way to get the romance content you crave.

Start your **FREE TRIAL** at
www.harlequinplus.com/freetrial.